A sharp nod was all I managed. One breath in, I lifted my right leg and slammed the heel of my boot into the door, banging it open.

Milly wore the same skin tight green dress she'd had on the previous day, and had her back to us. Four other people in the room faced us, hands raised. Shit, four witches against the two of us. The odds were definitely not in our favor.

The witches facing us wove spells, and based on the cannonballs rapidly headed in my direction, they knew to choose spells that wouldn't directly attack me, instead opting to hurt me with other things. Big nasty things that would smash my brains in if I wasn't careful.

PRAISE FOR SHANNON MAYER AND THE RYLEE ADAMSON SERIES

"If you love the early Anita Blake novels by Laurel K. Hamilton, you will fall head over heels for The Rylee Adamson Series. Rylee is a complex character with a tough, kick-ass exterior, a sassy temperament, and morals which she never deviates from. She's the ultimate heroine. Mayer's books rank right up there with Kim Harrison's, Patricia Brigg's, and Ilona Andrew's. Get ready for a whole new take on Urban Fantasy and Paranormal Romance and be ready to be glued to the pages!"

—*Just My Opinion Book Blog*

"Rylee is the perfect combination of loyal, intelligent, compassionate, and kick-ass. Many times, the heroines in urban fantasy novels tend to be so tough or snarky that they come off as unlikable. Rylee is a smart-ass for sure, but she isn't insulting. Well, I guess the she gets a little sassy with the bad guys, but then it's just hilarious."

—*Diary of a Bibliophile*

"I could not put it down. Not only that, but I immediately started the next book in the series, *Immune*."

—*Just Talking Books*

"*Priceless* was one of those reads that just starts off running and doesn't give too much time to breathe. . . . I'll just go ahead and add the rest of the books to my TBR list now."

—*Vampire Book Club*

"This book is so great and it blindsided me. I'm always looking for something to tide me over until the next Ilona Andrews or Patricia Briggs book comes out, but no matter how many recommendations I get nothing ever measures up. This was as close as I've gotten and I'm so freakin happy!"

—*Dynamite Review*

"Highly recommended for all fans of urban fantasy and paranormal."

—*Chimera Reviews*

"I absolutely love these books; they are one of the few Paranormal/urban fantasy series that I still follow religiously. . . . Shannon's writing is wonderful and her characters worm their way into your heart. I cannot recommend these books enough."

—*Maryse Book Review*

"It has the perfect blend of humor, mystery, and a slow-burning forbidden-type romance. Recommended x 1000."

—Sarah Morse Adams

"These books are, ultimately, fun, exciting, romantic, and satisfying. . . .Trust me on this. You are going to love this series."

—*Read Love Share Blog*

"This was a wonderful debut in the Rylee Adamson series, and a creative twist on a genre that's packed full of hard-as-nails heroines. . . . I will definitely stay-tuned to see what Rylee and her new partner get up to."

—Red Welly Boots

"*Priceless* did not disappoint with its colourful secondary characters, unique slant on the typical P.I. spiel, and a heroine with boatloads of untapped gifts."

—*Rabid Reads*

RAISING
INNOCENCE

Books by Shannon Mayer

The Rylee Adamson Series
Priceless
Immune
Raising Innocence
Shadowed Threads
Blind Salvage
Tracker
Veiled Threat
Wounded
Rising Darkness
Blood of the Lost

Rylee Adamson Novellas
Elementally Priceless
Tracking Magic
Alex
Guardian
Stitched

The Venom Series
Venom and Vanilla
Fangs and Fennel
Hisses and Honey

The Elemental Series
Recurve
Breakwater
Firestorm
Windburn
Rootbound

Contemporary Romance
High Risk Love
Ninety-Eight

Paranormal Romantic Suspense
The Nevermore Trilogy:
Sundered
Bound
Dauntless

Urban Fantasy
A Celtic Legacy Trilogy:
Dark Waters
Dark Isle
Dark Fae

RAISING INNOCENCE

A RYLEE ADAMSON NOVEL
BOOK 3

SHANNON MAYER

TALOS

New York

Talos Press books may be purchased in bulk at special discounts for sales promotion, corporate gifts, fund-raising, or educational purposes. Special editions can also be created to specifications. For details, contact the Special Sales Department, Talos Press, 307 West 36th Street, 11th Floor, New York, NY 10018 or info@skyhorsepublishing. com.

Talos Press® is a registered trademark of Skyhorse Publishing, Inc.®, a Delaware corporation.

Visit our website at www.talospress.com.

10 9 8 7 6 5 4 3 2 1

Library of Congress Cataloging-in-Publication Data is available on file.

Original illustrations by Damon Za www.damonza.com

Print ISBN: 978-1-940456-97-3

Printed in Canada

ACKNOWLEDGEMENTS

Raising Innocence, like all my books, wouldn't be possible without the amazing team of people around me. Melissa Breau and NL "Jinxie" Gervasio, my two editors who keep me from getting lazy, and always tell me the truth even when I don't want to hear it. Thank you ladies!

To Lysa Lessieur, my assistant, and public relations and marketing Queen you have not only made my life easier, you have given me an unexpected friendship and a shoulder to cry on when need be. You rock!

Okay, now to the nitty gritty. My readers are the reason I'm here, they are the reason I can write full time. I cannot thank you enough for your continued loyalty to me and Rylee, for your tweets, messages, and emails. I don't know if you realize how important you are to my writing life and I can't thank you enough.

I would be remiss if I didn't thank my hubby. Yes, I thank him in every book because he was the one to encourage me to chase my dreams of writing. So without him, there would be no Rylee, there would be no Alex, there would be no stories. He is the heart of all my tales, and the reason I believe that love conquers all.

CAST OF CHARACTERS

Rylee Adamson: Tracker and Immune
Liam O'Shea: FBI agent
Giselle: Mentored Rylee and Milly
Millicent: AKA Milly; Witch who is best friend to Rylee
John: Motel owner; friend of Rylee
Mary: Wife of John
India: A spirit seeker
Martins: O'Shea's FBI partner
Kyle Jacobs: Rylee's personal hacker
Doran: Daywalker and Shaman
Alex: A werewolf and friend of Rylee's
Berget: Rylee's little sister
Dox: Large pale blue-skinned ogre; Friend of Rylee
Maria: Mother of missing child
Don: Father of missing child
Louisa: Shaman
Eve: Harpy
Agent Valley: Senior in command in the Arcane Division of the FBI

1

I hung from the ceiling of my bedroom, my arm muscles trembling under the strain of holding up myself and the twenty-five pound sack of potatoes tied to my waist. The thick rope I'd wrapped around my right arm was frayed and rough, usually a good surface to grip, but not so much today. Sweat dripped from my body, making it hard to hang on. In nothing but a black tank top and stretchy jeans, I fought to keep up the pace I'd started with three hours before, my breathing harsh even to my own ears. I was desperate to stop my mind from going where it wanted to go. My workouts had always been an escape for me, but today even pushing my body to the edge of exhaustion wasn't keeping the flutter of anxiety in my gut still.

O'Shea still hadn't come back. It had been over a month since he'd been infected with the werewolf virus. A few months ago, I wouldn't have cared what happened to the FBI agent; he'd been a thorn in my ass for years. Then things had changed between us; he'd saved my life and I'd saved his. I'd thought I'd found a man who could stand with me in my world, be a part of my life. But maybe not. The supernatural world was a hard place to live, the learning curve deadly for most, especially for humans coming into it.

I grit my teeth and looked up to see how much higher I had to go. Three feet, not too far.

There hadn't even been any salvages to take my mind off Liam. Pretty bad when I was hoping for a child to go missing so I wouldn't have to think about one tall, dark, and dangerous man.

"Son of a bitch," I growled out, blinking away the sudden burst of nausea rolling up through my body. Oh, puking twenty-five feet up in the air was not going to happen.

With a pounding heart, and saliva filling my mouth as my gorge rose, I struggled to hold it together.

Visions of a fluffy bed and a darkened room where I could sleep for a week straight floated through my mind. If only my life were that easy to escape from. I wasn't sick—at least not physically; it was more a sickness of the heart. And that pissed me off. Weakness was not an option.

I only needed to swing a little to the right to grab the second rope hanging from the ceiling; then I could shimmy my way down. Only I rocked my body to the left, getting my momentum going—like pumping my legs on a swing. It took a couple of jerks left and right before I was close enough to grab the second rope with my left hand. The sack of potatoes continued to swing even after I stopped, jerking me hard to the left, and I slipped a few inches, the rope burning my arm. I bit the inside of my cheek until I tasted blood, and I clenched my fingers around the rope harder still. There was no way I was going to let go. I'd survive the fall—there were a few mats below me—but twenty-five feet up was a hell of a lot of pain and bruising just because I got tired and couldn't hang on.

As I let go of the first rope, a wave of fatigue hit me, and I slipped downward again, my overworked hands doing me no good in the way of grip. Desperation kicked in and I wrapped the rope around my legs—a cheat in my books for this particular exercise.

"Are you almost done?"

I glanced down at Milly, my former best friend and the best witch I knew. Even though I'd kicked her out of the house, chosen Alex over her, I could still say I was proud of her accomplishments. She could whip up a spell in no time, her natural talent needing very little help in the way of training. Of course, she had her flaws too. More than I cared to count. My eyes flicked over her; she was wearing a skin-tight black and green dress that hugged every inch of her curvy body, leaving nothing to the imagination. There was a bit more curve to her too, like she'd packed on some extra pounds. In the past, Milly's behavior hadn't bothered me—the way she did things or, more accurately, who she did things with. It was just a part of who she was. Lately, though, it had gotten under my skin, to the point where I couldn't bite my tongue. Then again, everything about Milly lately had me on edge.

"You're chubbing up, Milly. Maybe you should try working out on your feet instead of your back." I panted, frustrated by how much my routine was taking out of me.

Slipping and sliding, I let myself down the rope, the burn of the coarse material reminding me to grip a little more with my legs. Five feet up, I yanked the sack of potatoes up into the air so that it was at my eye level and then jumped, catching the bag on my way down.

Milly clapped, her expression one of self-indulgence, as she ignored my barb. "You done showing off? I need a hand getting the last of my boxes into my car."

Shrugging, I lowered the sack of potatoes to the ground and took a deep breath. "Yeah, sure."

The air between us was more than a little cool. She was still pissed at me. But I knew I'd made the right choice.

When I'd told her she had to go, she'd left immediately—she was never short on places to sleep—and had only just come back for the last of her things. We hadn't talked in the last few weeks and I felt the strain between us as if it were a living thing strangling what was left of our friendship to death. It hurt me to know how little she thought of me, of our history together. Apparently, O'Shea had been right—she'd meant more to me than I had to her.

With a frown, she tossed her long brown hair over one shoulder. "Hurry up, I have a date tonight. I don't want to be late."

I untied the rope from around my waist, jerking at it when it got stuck. "Then maybe you shouldn't have shown up in four-inch heels and a dress you're going to have to peel off. Shit, you're moving boxes, not stripping for me!"

Milly pouted, a move that helped her get her way with the male species, but didn't work on me. "It's the least you could do after picking that *werewolf* over me," she said, placing a hand on her hip, green eyes narrowing.

A black, contorted muzzle peeked around the edge of my bedroom door and one large amber eye blinked up at me. "Hiya witchy." He waved one paw at Milly. "Done peeing."

I held my hand out to him, and all two hundred pounds of werewolf came bounding into my room, banging against Milly's legs, which sent her sprawling to the floor, her spiked heels doing nothing to help her keep her balance. She screeched, I laughed, and Alex cringed against my legs. A weak, submissive werewolf, he was trapped between man and wolf, his body hunched and covered in black fur with silver tips; not to mention he had the mind of a two-year-old child.

But I had to admit he was one of the few good parts in my life, and seeing Milly sprawled out on the floor spluttering, I was glad once more I'd chosen him over her.

"It's okay, buddy." I patted his head. "Milly isn't mad; she's leaving."

That's where I was wrong. Milly pushed herself to her hands and knees, then used the door frame for support to stand. Her hands moved in a spell I recognized, the blackness surrounding her fingers—a tell I knew all too well.

I leapt toward her, slamming my hand over her mouth and tackling her to the floor. Being Immune had its perks, and this was one of them. The spell diffused against my skin, negating the effect she'd been going for.

"Oh, fuck no. You are not killing Alex over him knocking you down!"

She wrestled against me, but she never worked out, never thought about what would happen if she couldn't use her magic.

Shimmying up, I sat on her chest, pinning her arms to the floor with my knees. She bucked and writhed, and I finally lifted my hand from her mouth:

"Get the fuck off me!" Tears clung to her lashes and while I could understand her being angry, I didn't understand the crying.

"Milly, I wish you'd tell me what's going on," I said, not letting her up.

She flicked a finger and my bedroom lamp whipped at my head, catching me off guard. The ceramic base shattered against my skull, unbalancing me and giving her the edge she needed.

She scrambled away from me, crying, her makeup running down her face in long black streaks. Shit, now I felt bad. But I still couldn't let her kill Alex.

"I thought you were my friend, Rylee. But you aren't, you're no better than your parents, turning your back on the people who depend on you."

Fuck, now that was a low blow. I had to stop myself from physically cringing. "The friend I knew," I said, advancing toward her, "wouldn't try and kill Alex. Not for knocking her over. The friend I knew would tell me what was wrong with her. The friend I knew." I was yelling now, and Alex was howling from behind me, "wouldn't try to use my past against me!"

Milly cringed, then wiped her face, sniffling. "We aren't the same people anymore."

"You might not be." I turned my back on her to close my bedroom door and keep Alex out of her line of fire. "But I am. I still go looking for kids. That's what we swore we'd do. We took an oath."

Her head hung so that her chin nearly touched her chest. "I know."

"And you walked away from it like it was nothing!"

"I have other oaths—" She gulped back a sob and whatever else she was going to say, then shook her head.

Other oaths? To the Coven? It didn't really matter, not now. She'd made her choice.

Stomping my way past her, I went into her room and grabbed a box, the blood from my battered up hands smeared across the cardboard. The scent of roses caught me unawares—Milly's perfume.

A slight catch in my throat made me pause. I would not let her see me cry, not over this. Two strikes, she was out. The first time she had left me and Giselle it was for the Coven, and I saved her ass and brought her back. This time there would be no coming back; I could feel the difference.

Making my way back into the hallway, I was surprised to see her standing where I'd left her. "Come on, I'm not packing this all the way into Bismarck," I said.

She half-stumbled her way out to her car, a brand new white BMW. Someone was getting some serious sugar daddy time.

I all but threw the boxes into the back seat, wanting to be as far from her as possible. She was not my Milly, not the friend I'd grown up with. No, the stunning brunette in front of me was a stranger. A dangerous, deceptive stranger.

Turning my back on her, I headed back toward the rambling farmhouse, the sinking sun giving the perfect backdrop for a picture. Too bad cameras wouldn't work for me; this was a scene I needed to remember.

"Aren't you even going to say goodbye? And what about Giselle, I want to see her sometimes." Milly called after me, the echo of the lost girl she once was heavy in her voice.

My feet stilled and I rolled my shoulders. I'd said goodbye to her before, hoping she'd come back. She had, but she'd changed and not for the better.

"I'm not going to say goodbye." I lifted my eyes to hers, saw my own pain mirrored on her face. "And Giselle is none of your concern. I'll take care of her, no different than before."

Her body stiffened as if I'd struck her and the pain turned to anger, her lips parting as if to speak. I tensed, muscles prepped for a fight. If she wanted to get ugly, she knew my secrets, knew what would hurt me the worst both in the physical and metaphysical sense.

The air stilled, the ever-blowing wind of North Dakota stopping, as if it too held its breath. We stared at each other, eyes locked, the tension building until something had to happen. I sure as hell wasn't backing down, though. Her green eyes sharpened and I thought she would try and spell me. Shaking her head ever so slightly, she broke eye contact first. I let out a slow breath. The last thing I wanted to do was fight with her, because if it came down to it and she forced my hand, I would have to hurt her. Maybe even kill her. And despite everything, I still cared about her.

Milly ducked down into the BMW, the door slamming behind her. Within seconds she was peeling out of the driveway spitting gravel and dirt at me. The pebbles sprayed the bare skin on my arms, but I barely felt it. This was not like before, when she'd broken her ties with us for the Coven. I could feel it in my gut; Milly and I were done. The line had finally been drawn in the sand and we were on opposite sides.

Why then did I suspect this wouldn't be the last time she caused me grief?

2

Back inside the house, I let Alex out of my room and then cleaned up my hands, the raw skin biting at me with the antiseptic cleaner. Muttering under my breath, I wrapped my hands as best I could. It wouldn't take me long to heal. I wasn't near as fast as Alex, but still faster than the average human.

I cursed my way out to the main living area, my words stilling on my tongue as I took in the scene. Giselle sat in the corner of the window seat, staring out into the evening sky. Alex was curled up beside her, pointing at things.

Though they were at opposite ends of the spectrum in terms of supernatural abilities, the werewolf and my mentor had bonded over the last month. Maybe it was because in a weird way, they were the same, learning how to live in a body with a mind that was no longer their own. He was forever a child trapped inside his mismatched body, and she was only lucid at times.

While they sat and stared out the window, I sat on the floor, crossed my legs, and went to work on a routine, one that drained the shit out of me to practice. But it was necessary, especially with Alex.

With some effort, I'd learned over the last year to hold my Immunity back, just on my hands. Just enough to keep my Immunity from affecting Alex's collar and thus exposing him to the world as a werewolf. I did it without thinking for the most part, and the practicing was something I did now more when I was bored and had nothing better to do.

I played with it, peeling my Immunity up and over my wrists, sweating, but doing it. Because Giselle had said it was good for me to stretch myself and my talents, even if that meant trying things that seemed silly at times.

After an hour, I finally let my Immunity go back, flow over my hands. A slight tingle, and it was done.

Standing, I stretched, back popping one vertebrae after the other. "Giselle, are you hungry?"

Alex flipped himself over backwards, scrabbling across the hardwood floor, the silver tips of his fur catching the light. He slid to a stop at my feet and rolled huge amber eyes up to mine.

"Hungry, yes!"

Giselle chuckled to herself. "Socks, have you got your blue socks yet? You'll need them soon."

Helping her to her feet, I guided her into the kitchen. "No blue socks yet. But when I find them, I'll let you know."

"That's good. Blue socks. You need them for sure."

I settled her into a chair and heated up some leftovers. Nothing fancy, but at least it was home cooked. Alex dug in, alternating between using his claws and the fork, finally giving up and just using his mouth.

My mentor didn't eat; just sat there and stared. What was I going to do with her when I got my next salvage? There was no way I could take her with me when hunting for a kid. Even now, I had to lock her bedroom door at night; she'd wandered off three times in the last month. With the weather sitting well below freezing, it was a bad time to develop a thing for midnight walks in her nightshirt.

"Giselle, you need to eat." I held up fork with some food on it and pressed it against her mouth. She turned her head away like a naughty child. But I couldn't be angry; it wasn't her fault. The fault lay with the abilities she had to see what no one else could. The more she'd used her abilities, the more she was drained of her sanity; apparently it didn't happen to all of the supernaturals like her. But a lot of them, for sure, had the same trade-off. Not a very good exchange rate. Being a Tracker and an Immune, I didn't have drawbacks like that. Thank the gods.

I tried again to get her to eat, holding the fork up. She pushed it away. "Someone comes."

The sharp rap of knuckles on the front door sent a shiver of adrenaline through me. There were very few people I could call friends, and fewer still who'd show up unannounced.

My head and heart tripped over one another. O'Shea, it had to be O'Shea. Running full tilt to the door, I flung it open, breath catching in my throat.

Not O'Shea. But it was an FBI agent.

Agent Valley stood on my front porch looking up at me. Brown eyes flecked with green were definitely his best feature. He sported an overbite and an offset nose that looked as though it had been broken more than once. Jowly and a good four inches shorter than my 5'6, he wouldn't seem the type to be in charge. Yet, here he was, department head for the Arcane Arts division of the FBI. His perfectly pressed black suit and the file folder under his arm made him look like a travelling salesman.

Still, he was O'Shea's boss and my wannabe boss.

I didn't say anything, just stared down at him.

Finally, he cleared his throat. "May I come in? I have some information you might be interested in."

"About what?" I held the door, ready to slam it. Agent Valley wasn't a bad guy, just not exactly as good as I'd have liked. He'd tried to guilt me into coming to work for his division, and that was a real piss-off in my books.

"Some cases we are looking at. And I would like to speak to you about O'Shea."

Ah, here we go. He didn't know where O'Shea was, either. I could still Track him, but had only done so once. That one time was enough for me. He'd been close—in fact, I suspected he had something to do with the local werewolf pack's sudden loss of interest in Alex—but O'Shea was not a happy boy, his mental state fluxuating from rage to sorrow to blood lust, and then back through them all again. If I were to make a guess, I'd say that O'Shea could shift back and forth; his emotions were far too complex for him to have ended up like Alex. At least that was good. But I respected his choice. O'Shea wanted to figure this new part of his life out on his own. I wouldn't begrudge him that, though I missed him fiercely.

I waited another ten seconds before slowly opening the door and allowing the agent to step in. I didn't share my personal space well at the best of times—and this night certainly wasn't that.

Agent Valley made his way farther into the room, selecting the same chair he'd sat in last time he'd shown up unannounced, his feet not quite touching the floor.

"Are you going to sit down, so we can speak?" He opened the folder and drew out sheets of paper clipped together.

I folded my arms over my chest, tucking my bandaged hands away from sight. "No, I'll stand."

"So be it. But I will warn you, this is going to be a long conversation."

Snorting, one corner of my lips lifted. "I doubt that very much."

He seemed unfazed by my rudeness. One by one he laid out the paper-clipped piles on the table in front of him. "These children were all stolen from hospitals, all within the last two years."

I couldn't stop my ears from perking up. Why hadn't I heard about this? Something like this would have been all over the news. Bending, I scooped up the papers closest to me, thumbing through them. Six months old, in the hospital for not even twenty-four hours before going missing. Youngest of three. Sophia. That was almost a full two years ago; she must have been one of the first.

"There seems to be a strong correlation between the illnesses that the children came in to have treated and whether or not they get kidnapped," Agent Valley said, leaning back in his chair. I crouched to the ground and flipped through another pile. Age, four years. Oldest of two. Benjamin. There was nothing about why he was in the hospital.

Age, two-and-a-half. Only child. Jasmina.

Age, three weeks. One of two twins. Elana.

Age, five years. Middle of seven. Kent.

The list went on; there were over twenty children missing.

"Aren't you going to ask me what the correlation is?"

I spread the papers out, unable to stop myself from caring, even knowing that Agent Valley was manipulating me. "I suppose you'll tell me eventually. If not, it doesn't really matter. I can find them."

"So sure of yourself," he said softly.

I lifted my eyes to his. "It's one of the few things I'm sure of in my life."

Alex came trotting in from the kitchen, Giselle clinging to his collar. Neither one said anything to Agent Valley. They just went back to sitting on the window seat, staring out into the night sky.

The agent watched them, shaking his head ever so slightly. "I don't know how you can live with a werewolf."

My eyes narrowed, anger surging. What would he think if he knew O'Shea was a werewolf now? "Easier than living with some asshole with an overbite."

His face flushed from his head down to his collar, his lips tight, and a vein bobbing in the side of his face. For a brief second, I wondered if all FBI agents were required to have a vein in their face or neck that reacted when pissed off; like a mood thermometer.

Fuck, I really knew how to make people hate me. Was it just me or were all Trackers like that?

Maybe I should mellow out a little. At least, I could try. "What's the connection between all these kids?" I brushed my finger along the edge of their names, wishing I had a picture of one of them so I could Track them right now.

"They're terminal."

My brain froze, and I slowly lifted my head. Agent Valley was somber, his eyes full of grief.

"You mean like as in cancer?"

"Amongst other things."

I quickly scanned the papers and picked up the first one, Sophia. I held it out to him. "How long did she have?"

The agent took the paper and glanced at the name, not even consulting with another sheet before he answered. "Three months. Even if whoever took her had all the medical supplies they needed, she'd be dead by now."

Rocking on my heels, I looked at the papers with a new angle. "So you're telling me that not one of these kids is living? That they're all dead?"

"That's what I'm telling you."

I stood up and backed away from the agent and his piles of papers. There were times I went after a child and they were already dead, or they were killed before I could find them. Just one downside of being a Tracker. But going after these kids, this many dead? Shit, I wasn't sure I wanted to do that, to put myself through seeing that many parents grieving, to feel the depth of sorrow that only a child's death brought on. Besides, it wasn't like they didn't know the fate of their children. They knew they were dead, long past. Harsh, but true. A shiver ran through me and I could almost see the group of parents clinging to one another, crying, begging for mercy on their babies. No, this was not something I wanted to do.

"I think I'll pass. You know their fate. You don't need me."

Agent Valley leaned down and scooped the papers up one by one, slipping them back into his file folder. "I thought you might say that."

Moving back, I crossed my arms again, feeling like a fucking heel. But, there were times that even I wasn't strong enough. Weakness, hadn't I *just* bitched at myself over being weak? But this was different. The body I could conquer, the mind . . . all I could see in my mind were the parents, their sorrow, and then perhaps their condemnation. In my mind, they looked like my own parents as I was accused of murdering Berget, my little sister. They'd believed the worst of me and that had etched itself in my soul.

Agent Valley stood, but paused mid-step. "Have you heard anything from O'Shea?"

"No, he hasn't contacted me." That, at least, was the truth.

"But you could Track him, couldn't you?"

"I don't Track adults." Well, that was fudging it a little, but I owed Valley nothing.

He nodded. "I don't suppose I can ask you another question?"

Agent Valley was about to drop something on me. What, I could only guess; most likely something he thought would push me into a corner. Right then, I should have just said no, escorted him out and locked the door. But no, I had to nod and say, "Yeah, sure."

"We brought in a young hacker last week. He was the source of a major leak in our department, and was caught selling information on our confidential Arcane Arts division. Of course, we stopped him before it was able to get out to the world via the black market."

My muscles tightened and my brain was screaming at Kyle. The little prick, after I paid him so fucking well? Now at least I knew where the printout I'd had disappeared to, the little bastard! I'd never even had a chance to go over the papers on the AA division before they'd gone missing while I was on a salvage. Kyle must have snuck out to my place, knowing that I'd be indisposed. But why wouldn't he have just hacked in and re-printed the information?

The next time I saw him I would have to ask; then, I would kick his ass into next year for crossing me.

"Hmm. I don't see what this has to do with me." I stilled my nerves, forced myself to stand relaxed and at ease. Jail was not somewhere I wanted to end up; I'd been on the wrong end of the law once in my life. Once was enough, thank you very much.

"Well, I just thought you'd like to know."

"That's not a question," I said, my voice even and calm.

"Isn't it?"

We were in a stare off, him waiting for me to break. It would be a freaking happy day in Hell when I didn't win a staring competition. I shrugged. "You are one strange little man."

He glanced away. Point for Rylee. I had to give him credit. He was pretty good at trying to get what he wanted without full on asking for it. But it wouldn't work with me.

"Can you at least tell me if he's alive?"

Back to O'Shea again.

"Now that's a question." I leaned one hip against the wall. "Yes. He's alive."

Agent Valley nodded. "Is he coming back?"

That was an even better question, one I'd like the answer to as well.

I took in a long slow breath, let it out as I formed words I hated to say. "I don't know."

The agent nodded and then headed for the front door; he made it all the way there before turning around, a smile on his lips. He was way too happy after I'd just turned him down. I felt the first niggling of fear along the back of my neck; he'd been holding back.

"It's a shame you aren't interested in the case."

I nodded and gave him a tight-lipped smile, but said nothing else.

Tapping his folder against his leg, his eyes seemed to twinkle, his hand on the open door.

Shit, here it comes.

"The team's main source of help is in the hospital, too sick to move anymore."

My eyebrows lifted, confusion flitting through me. "And this would be important to me why exactly?"

Agent Valley smiled and I felt the hook set in mouth as he said, "Because he's a Tracker."

3

I couldn't stop my jaw from dropping. Agent Valley said nothing, stepped out onto the porch, and shut the door firmly behind him.

There had never been another Tracker that I'd known about, no one to learn from, no one to tell me how not to do things, or even what other things I might be able to do. I couldn't let this pass by me, even if he was bluffing. Shit, shit, shit.

Grabbing at the door I flung it open to see the agent smiling up at me. "Shall we start again?"

Flustered and irritated that he'd played me like a freaking harp, I stepped back to let him come back inside. Once again seated in my living room, he held out his hands.

"I thought you might turn me down, this isn't the kind of case you typically go after. You like to find them alive, not long past their expiry date."

Snorting, I sat on the edge of the coffee table, the wood corner pressing into my thigh. "After finding your first half-rotten child corpse, you wouldn't be so eager to go after them, either."

He blanched.

That had been one of my earliest salvages, and it had left me with nightmares and flashbacks for weeks. Even now, I could still smell the putrid mix of decaying meat and baby powder to cover it up. No, that was not something I willingly went after. If a kid was missing, and I took on the salvage and they died before I could get to them, I did my best to bring them home. But taking on a salvage willingly, knowing that the kid was gone? Nope, not as fun as it sounds.

Agent Valley eyed me up and down. "You are not what I expected, from what O'Shea reported, I thought you'd be more of a hard ass."

"Yeah, he would say that," I muttered. "Listen, what about this Tracker, why can't he go after them?"

"Like I said, he's in the hospital. Dying. Lung cancer, I believe." He handed me a piece of paper with a name on it I didn't recognize, stats, but again no picture.

Jack Feen. Age forty-nine, single, red hair, blue eyes. Tracker. Seeing the Tracker's stats on paper made it more real to me for some reason.

"Where is he?"

"That's where things get tricky."

I lifted my eyes to the agent, expecting him to squirm under my glare. I didn't like this game he was playing with me. "What do you mean, tricky?"

"You see, it isn't just the FBI on this case."

Brilliant.

He cleared his throat, seeming to almost choke on the words. "Interpol has asked for our help. Their Tracker is down and they want to borrow ours. You."

I shot up, my voice rising sharply. "What the hell? You've been telling your buddies that I'm on payroll? You think you can pawn off my services like I'm some sort of high-priced bird dog?"

Alex gave a soft woof. I'd almost forgotten he was there, he'd been so quiet. A look over at him and Giselle, seeing their eyes look to me for reassurance, calmed me down. No good would come of getting riled up; I didn't have to do what Agent Valley asked of me. But I knew I'd never find the other Tracker if I didn't help him.

Son of a bitch, he was a sneaky bastard.

"Where?"

Agent Valley continued to smile. "London. All the children were snatched from hospitals in London, and it's where Jack Feen is dying. You won't have much time. The doctors are saying he's got weeks at best."

London. How the hell was I supposed to get there in a giant piece of technology that could flick off at the drop of the hat simply because I was too close to it?

I smiled, seeing a roadblock he likely hadn't considered. "And how would you like me to get there? Paddleboat? Swim? Click my heels together three times?"

He continued to grin, and I knew I'd finally met someone who might outmaneuver me. O'Shea had been persistent, had intimidated me and never backed down. But this man, this short, dumpy, ugly little man, had an answer for everything.

"We've outfitted a Boeing 747 with the proper displacement materials to keep your vibrations from setting off the equipment. You can fly out in three days, and be in London with plenty of time to visit Jack."

"Vibrations?" What the fuck was he talking about?

"Our scientists have determined that it is specific vibrations that supernaturals give off that interfere with technology. I'm not going to explain it now. Suffice to say that we understand the cause and have a way to block the resulting problems."

This was news to me. But it made sense. I swallowed hard, my mind racing with possibilities. He wanted me to go, needed me to. I'd lay money he'd already told Interpol that I was coming. Hmm. I could use this to my advantage. Let's see how he liked the tables being turned.

"Then I want a few things besides the usual pay cut."

He nodded as if expecting this. He hadn't seen anything yet.

I held up one finger. "I need a care nurse here twenty-four-seven while I'm away, for Giselle. Someone who is familiar with dementia *and* the supernatural."

Pursing his lips, he pulled a phone from his breast pocket and scanned through it. "Yes, that can be managed. We have someone in our AA division that is familiar with both."

"I want to pick my back-up."

"That's fine. I don't have a problem with that."

Smiling, I leaned back. "Eve is coming with us. I can make her small with a spelled anklet that Milly left for me."

Agent Valley's jaw clenched. "You want to bring a Harpy with you."

"She'll be about the size of a hawk. Fits right into the plane with no problem." I continued to smile—this was kinda fun. Almost as much fun as I had playing with O'Shea when he'd been trying to bring me down. Almost.

The agent gave a sharp nod. "She can be controlled, I assume?"

"Of course. She's got all her mental faculties. She's young, but bright." I smiled. I was going to make him pay for twisting me around. "And Alex comes with me, too."

Alex jumped up at the sound of his name. "Coming?"

"Yup, we're going to London," I said as Agent Valley sputtered.

"That's too much; you can't bring a werewolf to London. Impossible. Bad enough that you want to bring a Harpy!"

Grinning down at the werewolf, who rolled on his back at my feet, I rubbed his belly with one foot. "Alex is a part of my search team. He helps keep me safe, amongst other things."

Alex wiggled on his back, balancing on his spine with feet straight up in the air. "Alex going to London, Alex going to London," he chanted, wrapping it all up with a howl of "Keeping Rylee saaaaaaafe."

Agent Valley stood, his face red. "You can't bring a werewolf to London!"

I laced my fingers in my lap and said quietly, "Then I'm not going."

His jaw went tight and I knew I had him. Still, he didn't answer right away. We had a second stare off, and again, I won, his eyes flicking away from mine to look out the window.

"I won't promise you anything. There are other factors I have no control over," Valley said.

"Not my problem. Alex and Eve come with me or I'm not going."

"I heard you the first time. I will do my best." Agent Valley narrowed his eyes. "You can keep him on a leash, and hide him with that collar of yours, correct?"

Fuck, how much did he know about me and Alex? "Of course. I'm not going to go running around London announcing I have a werewolf." What did he think I was, an idiot?

"One more thing," I said.

The agent was standing back up, and I wanted to be sure we understood each other before I dove into this.

"What is it, Ms. Adamson?"

Ah, getting formal now, that was a good sign. Meant he was finally taking me seriously.

"This doesn't mean I'm working for you. Nor does it mean I'm going to do things your way. Consider this a one-time contract to find those kids."

His eyes narrowed, anger flitting across his face before he smoothed it away. "Anything else?"

"I'll be sending you an invoice through my manager." Okay, Charlie wasn't my manager per se, but close enough.

Shaking, Agent Valley gave a sharp nod, turned and headed once more for the front door.

"We'll send a car round for you in three days; your flight leaves at noon on the seventeenth."

"I can't leave until I know for sure someone is here with Giselle."

"I will have someone here before your flight."

I felt like I'd scored a major victory as the door clicked shut behind the FBI agent. Slumping against the opposite wall, I stared at the door. I was leaving for London in three days, with Alex and Eve. Better than that, I was going to meet a Tracker.

The rush of excitement that zinged through me left me shaking with excess energy. Milly was going to freak when I . . . No, Milly wouldn't know about this. The excitement drained and I frowned down at my shoes. Ah, fuck it. I was going to celebrate anyway.

Jogging into the kitchen, I dialed Charlie's number on my old rotary phone, the tick of the dial clicking softly as it spun around with each number.

He answered with a "Hello, me lassie! No new salvages for yous. Good and bad, eh?"

"Right now it's a good thing. Charlie, come on over, I need someone to clink glasses with."

He let out a shout. "Gods be praised, yous going to start drinking!"

Laughing, I cradled the phone against my shoulder. "Don't get excited, I'll be drinking orange juice."

"Bah, you don't know what you be missing, lassie. But I'll be there in a jiff."

I hung up and two minutes later there was a knock on the door. That was one of the things about Brownies. They could use doorways and windows as jumping points. Pretty handy, if you asked me.

Dressed in blue jeans and a button down shirt, he sported a black bowler that truly did not match the long fur coat he wore. Open, of course, like he'd thrown it on and scrambled to get here. Then again, it could have been because he was trying to hide the fact he was missing a leg. It had happened a long time before I'd ever met him and he wouldn't talk about it. Not even when he got drunk on ogre beer.

Charlie was about three feet tall, and I scooped him up easily into a hug.

"What the hells has happened to yous, lassie?" He grunted as I put him down. His eyes searched my face, as if he thought to see something stamped on my forehead.

"I'm excited." I wasn't sure I could describe it to him. My whole life I'd been alone, the only Tracker Giselle had ever known, and no one I'd met had ever met another. Maybe Doran had, from his cryptic words, but I wasn't so sure I'd trust the Daywalker Shaman to tell me the truth. Every other supernatural was a part of a group, even vampires, the few there were, had each other. But Trackers—I'd never known another one. For years I'd thought that was always how it was going to be.

In one long rambling, high-speed sentence, I spilled. "There's another Tracker in London and I'm going to meet him in three days and I can't even believe that this is happening and I have no one else to tell 'cause I kicked Milly out and the FBI is going to have someone take care of Giselle while I'm gone and they're even going to pay us!"

Charlie looked at me, his eyebrows lowered, and he lifted his hands as if to slow me down. "Easy, lass. Are yous sure yous not been fed anything strange? Ogre beer, perhaps?"

I scrubbed my face with my hands. "No, sorry, I just . . . I just thought I was alone."

The Brownie smiled up at me. "Yous never been alone, Rylee. Yous got lots who love you. Me for one. The big blue ox down south, and ogre's don't give their loyalty easy like. Alex here, of course, he'll never leave yous."

We headed into the kitchen. "I know that. I don't mean, it's just . . . Charlie, if there were no other Brownies, how would you know all the things you could or couldn't do?"

He opened his mouth as if to argue, but paused. "Damn me, I guess I wouldn't. Well, no, some things I'd figure out."

I poured him a shot of Milly's best whiskey and handed the glass to him, then poured a glass of orange juice for myself.

"Exactly. Once I meet this other Tracker, I'll finally have someone to show me all the things I can do. I've no doubt there's more to my abilities than what I've figured out on my own. Maybe there's nothing else, but at least I'll know."

Charlie climbed onto the kitchen chair so we were eye level, his glimmering with tears. He'd lost everything, his wife and children. So the idea that we could help others find their kids, well, it was almost as much a drive for him as it was for me.

"And then yous can help even more of the wee ones with what you learn. Ah, I see now why you be so excited."

Nodding, I clinked my glass to his. "Exactly."

4

"**E**ve, I wouldn't ask you to do this if it wasn't important," I said as I stared up at the juvenile Harpy pacing around my backyard. She was well over a thousand pounds, with the beak, wings, and talons of a bird, but her upper body was human-looking, complete with all the trappings of being female. Lower body was all bird, her massive wings set just behind the blending of skin and feathers.

She'd flown back to North Dakota as soon as I'd called down to her, Dox passing on the message for me. Most surprising was that she'd brought presents for each of us; a fossilized bone for Alex that he'd been chewing since she'd given it to him, an obsidian blade for me, and a necklace for Giselle. That last was the most disturbing because it had not come from Eve.

It had come from Doran.

I held it for a long time before handing it over to Giselle, unsure of what it would do, if anything. She'd just let it fall from her fingers, not even watching when it hit the ground. So that was that.

Alex, his new bone, and Giselle were curled up in several blankets on the back porch, watching us. Alex gave Eve a double thumbs up while Giselle continued to mutter about blue socks.

"Rylee, it isn't that I don't want to help you," Eve said, as she continued to stride about, her clawed feet turning the snow and ice into a slurry of pale brown mud. "But the idea of being spelled is . . . ." She turned large golden eyes to me. She'd been held captive by a Coven of black witches when I'd first met her. Things hadn't gone so well for the witches, but they hadn't gone so well for Eve and her sisters, either. Only Eve was left, courtesy of me and my blades.

"I understand," I said, laying the clasp in front of her. "I wouldn't ask if I didn't think it was necessary. You know Europe and the supernaturals there better than I do. "

That was the truth. She'd lived there in her early years before coming to America with her sisters. Or, more accurately, until they took off from Europe because their Clutch evicted them.

Eve fluttered her wings. She'd been training with Eagle, a tribal Guardian in New Mexico, for over a month. Already I could see the changes in her, maturity that hadn't been there before, not just jumping into things, overall a better control of her emotions—something essential to a Harpy, at least as far as I was concerned. Whatever training she was getting, it was doing her a world of good. Perhaps I should have let her stay with Eagle, should have done this salvage on my own.

No, I couldn't trust the FBI to actually help me, and the gods only knew what I'd be facing over there. Without Milly or O'Shea at my side, I knew enough to know that I couldn't do this run alone. Call it a gut feeling, intuition, or whatever the hell you want, everything about this run screamed at me to take all the ammunition I could. Not a good sign, but one I would deal with.

With a heavy sigh, Eve bobbed her head once. "Yes, I will wear the anklet. Perhaps we could try it now, before the moment comes that I must wear it? Then I will be ready for whatever changes it puts on me."

I smiled up at her. "You have grown up a lot, Eve."

She blushed and clacked her beak. "Eagle is a good mentor, a good flyer. I like him." The flush deepened and warning bells went off in my head. Shit, if she had a crush on the tribal Guardian, that would not end well. He would only be around long enough to make sure his Shaman gained enough strength to take care of herself. What was I going to do with a broken-hearted Harpy? I shook off those thoughts. No point in going there just yet. Besides, she was young; she would grow out of a silly crush on Eagle. I hoped.

"As long as I'm holding the anklet, the spell won't kick in," I explained to Eve. I bent down to put the diamond and ruby studded clasp around her leg, just above her claws.

"Since it's not just an illusion, I have no idea if it will hurt or not. It shouldn't, though," I said, fingers slipping off the clasp. I stood up, and took a step back. "You feel anything?"

Eve shook her head. "It's cold against my skin, but I feel—wait, it's starting to heat up."

That was a good sign.

It didn't last.

Eve screamed. Wings outstretched, she let out a screech and fell to the ground, her body convulsing as her eyes nearly bugged out of her head, her voice sounding as if she were being strangled.

"Rylee!"

Alex barked, high-pitched, full of fear, and even Giselle let out a moan that added to the energy swirling around us.

Fuck, what was going on? I ran to Eve's side and a sharp talon whipped over my head. I dropped to the ground, rolling across the crunchy snow to get close to her.

"Hold still!"

"I can't!" She screeched, wings thumping the ground hard enough that I anticipated the crunch of bones, or at the very least the sickening snap of her pinion feathers.

Her talons swept by me again, brushed along my back and sliced open my jacket. Razor-sharp was a freaking understatement. I lunged forward, now well within the danger zone of her claws, and wrapped myself around her leg. Riding her leg, I reached down and grasped the anklet, stopping the flow of magic with a simple touch of my hand.

Her wings stilled and she let out a low moan, her body going limp in the snow. We both lay there, still as could be; I was unwilling to move and chance losing contact with the anklet. I suspected she was hurt, but I wasn't ready to ask that just yet.

Panting, she shifted her weight and stared down at me. "I have never felt so much pain; it was as if a thousand flaming hot knives were burrowing under my skin to flay me alive."

There was no question as to what was going to happen now.

"I'm taking this off," I said, my hands moving to unclasp the anklet.

"No, perhaps it is just the normal discomfort of shifting into a smaller form. Now that I'm ready for it, I can take it. The pain just caught me off guard," she said, blinking back tears. Shit, this was too much to ask.

"No, I'm taking it off. None of Milly's spells cause pain, not unless—"

Giselle's voice curled around me. "Unless she wanted to cause pain. Or death. Or a theft of powers."

A quick snap and I'd unlatched the anklet. Giselle was right. I took a close look at the anklet. There was something different about it. I counted the diamonds and the rubies. The number was the same, but they were in a different pattern, so subtle I didn't notice it. Milly must have switched out the anklet she had originally given me at some point for this one, maybe while I'd been in New Mexico. She did this on purpose. A part of my brain was stunned, absolutely fucking stunned at the lengths Milly was going to in order to get her way. When had she resorted to death spells as the answer to her so-called problems? More importantly, why? It didn't make sense, at least not with the girl I knew, the girl I'd thought of as my sister. Another part of my brain wasn't so forgiving. The Tracker in me saw only a threat to my charges, and I was leaning heavily to agreeing with that portion.

I was going to kill her.

And I didn't mean in I'm-going-to-beat-your-ass-until-you're-black-and-blue kind of way. More like I'm-going-to-run-you-through-with-my-sword-you-fucking-piece-of-white-trash-slut.

"Eve, are you okay?" I asked softly, shame nipping at my heels and smothering my anger for a brief moment. She'd trusted me and I'd let her down. But I would make it right.

"I'm okay, Rylee. You couldn't have known."

With a tight grip on the anklet, I shook my head. "I didn't know, but now I do."

I strode around the side of the house, the snow slippery under my feet. With a sharp jerk I yanked the door to my weapons stash open and stepped down into the converted cool storage-turned armory.

Could I really do this? Could I really hunt down my best friend? Yes, I decided. She hadn't left me any choice.

There was only one thing I needed. No, make that two. I slipped on my back sheath, which would hold my two swords under my jacket, and settled the weapons. There wasn't much time, less than twenty-four hours before my flight left for London. But it was enough to find Milly and end this.

She wanted those closest to me dead for some reason, and the only way to protect them was to kill her. Maybe she thought I couldn't do it. My heart clenched and I fought a sudden wave of grief, tears working their way to the edge of my eyes.

I would not cry, damn it!

Dashing a hand across my face, I sucked in a sharp breath, smelling the still lingering scent of musty old vegetables mixed with leather soap and dust. *Pull yourself together. She'll kill you if you go in weak.*

What had happened to her? Was she possessed? But even if that was the case, I had to end this. Possession, unlike the movies show you, is not reversible. Once you have a demon truly possess you, there's no going back.

Letting my breath out, I silenced the side of me that wanted to believe Milly could be reasoned with, the child in me that wanted her best friend to always be her best friend. That was not my life. I had to protect those who looked to me for safety.

Grabbing a couple of bottles of salt water, I headed back up the stairs, kicked the sloped door shut behind me, and strode to my Jeep.

Stashing the salt water behind my seat the sound of the passenger door opening brought my head up. I looked up expecting Alex, surprised to see Giselle opening the passenger door.

"What are you doing?" I made a move as if to stop her.

"Milly is as much my responsibility as yours."

Gods, how I wished that Giselle wouldn't have become lucid right then. If there was any moment when I prayed for her mind to lose its connection with the real world, that was it. The moment that one of her 'daughters' would kill the other.

"Giselle, you can't come with me. Your powers have drained you, and I can't keep us both safe."

She smiled over at me, a wry twist to her lips. "For once, you will listen to me, stubborn Tracker."

My eyebrows went up. I always listened to her. Really.

Giselle slid into the passenger seat, her body moving with a stiffness that made her look older than she truly was.

"There are a few last lessons I would give you. And now your friend Doran has given me the chance to hold the madness at bay long enough to do so." She held up the rainbow opal now hanging around her neck.

Only a month had gone by since I'd worn a similar opal, one of the fire variety, to keep some nasty demon venom from freezing my ass off. It's a long story, but the crux of it is this: the longer I wore the fire opal, the more powerful the kickback if it came off.

I licked my lips. "Giselle, what happens when you take the opal off?"

With one swift move, she buckled herself into my Jeep, her eyes staring straight ahead.

"You know what will happen. It is time. I am more a burden than I am a help."

"I can't let you do this," I said, my heart thumping painfully, as if it wanted to beat its way out of my chest. She couldn't mean to do this, not now.

Giselle turned to face me, her eyes softening. "You have no say. I am your mentor still, and you will listen to me this one last time. It is my wish, and you *will* honor it." She clapped her hands together, ending that line of conversation as she had so many times when I was still a teenager.

Uncertainty flared within me, but I did as she said, climbed in my Jeep, and started the engine.

If this was how I was to honor her, then so be it.

5

"Now, Rylee, what does Milly know about you?" Giselle asked as I drove into Bismarck. I was Tracking Milly and could feel the threads of her life humming on the far side of the city.

"Everything," I said, eyes focused on the road.

"Be specific."

I grunted and my lips curled upward. This felt like the beginning, when Giselle would school me on everything and anything she could. Always the same. Be specific.

"She knows I'm a Tracker, that I can trace her wherever she is. She knows I'm an Immune and that her magic won't touch me unless presented in an indirect manner." I thought for a minute, a niggling idea worming its way to the front of my brain. "Why do you think this is your responsibility? And don't tell me because you helped train us both. Because it's more than that, isn't it?"

Giselle shifted in her seat. "Milly has tasted of darkness each time I've read her. Even in the beginning it was there, but then only a seed. Always, I hoped that she would purge the darkness."

I caught her shake her head out the corner of my eye.

"But I believe now that she was placed with us for a purpose. Perhaps for the very thing you are going to do now. This could be a trap."

Frowning, I forced myself to think of Milly no longer as Milly, but as one of those supernaturals who had to be put down for the betterment of the world. I swallowed the burning lump in my throat, fought the emotions that would be the death of me.

"You mean," I said, "that she was placed with us to gain my trust so she could kill me?"

"You are going after her, aren't you?"

"Yes."

"And she is the most powerful witch the world has known in centuries."

Gooseflesh rose up over my body. "I didn't know that. I knew she was strong, but . . ."

The steady tap of Giselle's fingernails on the middle console drummed in rhythm with some beat I couldn't hear. "How could you not?"

I shrugged, intensely embarrassed. "I knew she was good, knew that the Coven wanted her at all costs. But she never talked about the level of her skills. Neither did you, for that matter."

My mentor let out a sharp barking laugh. "Truly, I was blinded by my love for her, as were you. She was the perfect undercover agent."

"I guess the only question is, who is she working for?" My mind went to Faris, the vampire who'd sought my favors in his own perverted way. First, he tried to kiss me, then kill me, and then he, in a round-about way, saved my life. But how would Milly fit in with him?

Or was it someone else? Fuck, the last thing I needed was someone else gunning for me.

We drove in silence for a few minutes before I blurted out what I was thinking. "Why did you use your abilities so much, if you knew that you would lose your mind?"

Giselle turned to me, placing a hand over mine. "Pull off at the next exit."

The off-ramp seemed to appear at her command, and I flicked on my blinker and took it without hesitation. With a few minor directions, Giselle guided us to a dirt road covered with a thin dusting of snow that led out to the badlands where we'd be able to talk uninterrupted.

"Stop here."

I put the Jeep in park, but left it and the heat running, and then turned to face my mentor, the only person who'd had enough faith in me to believe I hadn't killed my little sister. Giselle was the one who'd taught me to trust again, that it was okay to hold tight to those closest to you. She'd also taught me to fight, kill, and do what was right, no matter the cost. And a part of me felt betrayed by the fact that she would willingly give up her mind, she would willingly leave me behind. I was once more feeling abandoned by someone who should have stood by me.

She turned to me, her hazel eyes so clear and free of the madness that for a moment, I forgot it had ever happened.

"We are each called to this world, Rylee, for a purpose. Some of us find it, like you. Others are not so lucky. Not until I met you and Milly did I find my purpose, and it was shortly after that when the madness began."

I sucked in a sharp breath. "I didn't know that it started that long ago."

She clasped her hands in her lap. "Yes, I hid it well, but I knew it was only a matter of time before I lost control. So I chose to give you two girls all I had, and every ounce of my abilities I could share with you, I did. You were my purpose in this world. My job was to protect, train, and love you. All three of which I did without hesitation."

My jaw hurt from clenching it tight and I thought she was done, but she went on, and finally the tears slipped out of my control down my face.

"You have the best of me in you, as if you were my daughter in truth." She smiled somewhat ruefully as she reached out and swiped a tear off my cheek. "You also have some of my bad traits, but those I will let you discover on your own."

Her eyes softened even further. "But for me, I know I have done the world a great service by loving you, by teaching you what I could, and by setting you on the path of being a Tracker in truth; one that lets her heart lead her, and the world be damned."

"Giselle, I don't want to be alone. Not again," I whispered, ashamed at admitting the old deep-seated fear, even to her.

"You aren't alone, though, are you? The strength of your character, the drive in you—it draws those to you that will fight for you, with you, and perhaps sometimes even smack you upside the head when you get mouthy."

A teary laugh escaped me, and she laughed along with me. Scrubbing my face, I sniffed back my grief. I would lose her before this day was done, I could feel it in my bones, and it scared the shit out of me.

"Now, we must go. Because if I'm right, Milly will be waiting for us," Giselle said, her eyes darkening with anger.

I put the Jeep into drive, the engine rumbling smoothly as I headed back to the Interstate. Knowing Milly was going to try and kill us was one thing, just like knowing that the night would come after the setting sun. And just like the night, I knew it would only be a matter of time before she succeeded.

That was, unless I beat her to it.

We spent the rest of the drive reminiscing, talking about old times, good times and bad, that we'd had— our final goodbye, and we both knew it. Without meaning to, my foot eased off the gas pedal, extending our time together, even if only for a few additional minutes. It would never be enough, though, not for me.

Tracking Milly was easy, something I did without even thinking, really. She was the first person I'd ever Tracked on purpose, the first person's whose life threads had hummed inside my skull, a vibration all their own.

I followed her threads through Bismarck to the northeast side of town. There wasn't much here, at least nothing that should have drawn her. She'd always loved the glitz and glamour of the city life.

"Stop thinking about her as your friend, Rylee."

A long slow breath in helped to calm me, then I let it out and, with it, let go of Milly once and for all.

Milly's threads drew me to a beautiful office building, newer, but with architectural touches that showed a modern design with a nod to the past. Squinting my eyes and using my second sight, I could just see the faint outlines of what had to be the Coven's symbol, a full moon with the faint image of a wolf inside it, on the front door. What the hell, why not storm the Coven's main building? One last hurrah for Giselle and me. The witch was inside, resting, by the feel of things. Not sleeping, but relaxing. I had no way of knowing how many other Coven members there were.

"Maybe you should wait here," I said, thinking about how to get to the top of the three-story building and past any number of Coven members with Giselle, who was frail on a good day.

"I can bloody well walk. I'm not dead yet," she snapped at me.

Oh, there was one of those bad traits she mentioned. A smile flitted across my lips, but disappeared as I stepped out of the Jeep.

The ever-blowing wind of North Dakota seared my eyeballs, making them tear up. Damn it all.

Blindly, I groped in the back seat, grabbed the two bottles of salt water, and then shut the door with my hip. I wasn't worried about being heard or detected. I was an Immune, unable to be detected or affected directly with magic; it was a perk that went with the territory.

"Do you have a plan?" Giselle asked.

"The usual."

"So you mean no plan."

"Exactly."

Plans went awry and people fell apart. In my mind, it was better to always go in hot, and adjust yourself as the shit hit the fan.

We walked to the front door and I hesitated. I might not set off any alarm system, but Giselle would. I glanced over at her and she lifted a single eyebrow at me. We'd done this many times before she'd lost her sanity and we needed very few actual words to communicate. I handed her the two bottles of salt water first.

Then I crouched down so I could carry her on my back. My crossed sword sheath dug into me, but it was a minor irritant. Did my Immunity flow over Giselle like a cloak?

Fucked if I know, but it was the best we could do with what we had.

Giselle's ability lay in reading people, seeing the future, seeing the past. But she had once been a wicked ass fighter. She'd learned to fight because, like me, her abilities didn't provide the sort of power that someone like Milly had. We were both fighters in the physical sense and could kick Milly's ass around town in that arena; our one major advantage over her. Of course, the chances were good that the bitch witch wasn't alone. Nor did it help that Giselle was so out of shape, and wasted from the madness.

The doorknob was cool under my touch and I twisted it with care, easing the door open. Poking my head in, I spotted stairs across the lobby, and no one waiting for us.

Yet.

Shifting Giselle on my back, I walked as fast as I could across the lobby, doing my best to soften the sound of my boots on the marble floor.

"Opulent for a Coven who has no ties to the world, isn't it?" Giselle noted, her voice low.

I was thinking along the same lines. Milly had claimed the Coven had no ties with the secular world, that they were woefully ignorant of the humans, and even at times, other supernaturals. But this place didn't give me that feeling, not by a long shot.

There was even a computer at the desk, which meant that there were humans here.

We made it all the way to the third floor before I put Giselle down and pulled my two blades out of their sheaths. There was only a single door between us and Milly, and my heart pounded. I could do this; I had to.

My hands were slick with sweat, my muscles trembled, and it wasn't the climb of the stairs that was doing it.

Giselle reached over and put a hand on my forearm. "Steady, Rylee. This must be done. Much as we hate it."

A sharp nod was all I managed. One breath in, I lifted my right leg and slammed the heel of my boot into the door, banging it open.

Milly wore the same skin tight green dress she'd had on the previous day, and had her back to us. Four other people in the room faced us, hands raised. Shit, four witches against the two of us. The odds were definitely not in our favor.

The witches facing us wove spells, and based on the cannonballs rapidly headed in my direction, they knew to choose spells that wouldn't directly attack me, instead opting to hurt me with other things. Big nasty things that would smash my brains in if I wasn't careful. Shit, shit, shit! Milly had told them.

"They know!" Was all I managed before spinning to dodge the cannonball that came spinning toward my head.

Giselle threw the two bottles of salt water, one right after the other, but only doused a single witch. Not enough.

Milly had set the trap, and we'd walked right into it.

"Giselle, get out of here!" I yelled, knowing that she wouldn't leave, but I had to try.

Milly moved away from me as I dodged and ducked the cantaloupe-sized iron balls. It looked like they were throwing two or three each, six balls zinging around the room at a speed I could only just keep ahead of. I tried to keep track of Milly while I dodged the balls, but it was impossible to do both. Dodging the balls became my main focus.

I hit the ground, rolling toward the closest witch, a man who stood about my height with short blond hair. That was all I registered before I grabbed his ankle and jerked him off his feet. He hit the ground with a grunt, two cannonballs dropping with him, and I moved on to the next witch. If I could disrupt their spells enough, we had a chance.

Not a good chance, but a chance nonetheless.

"Rylee, left," Giselle yelled.

I jerked my body to the left, three cannonballs slicing through the air where I'd been. I flipped up to my feet and ran at the one closest to me, my right sword slicing through the air, taking off her arm at the elbow. She screamed, her face a blur to me as I spun.

One of the cannonballs caught me, slamming into my lower back with a force that knocked the wind out of me and sent me sailing across the room. I hit the far wall, stars dancing in front of my eyes as the pain in my back spread. My fingers and toes tingled, and I could move them, but not fast enough.

The cannonballs caught me then. As they hit me the spells diffused, but that wasn't enough to stop the impacts, although apparently it was enough to let the witch turn her attention to the cannonballs her fellows had dropped.

Bones crunched. I felt them snap and twist. I slumped, unable to dodge what was coming at me. Pain flared but disappeared as the next ball hit me, leaving a new impression. Fast and hard, I couldn't see them pinned face-first against the wall, but I sure as shit on a troll could feel them.

I was so fucked.

"Enough!" Giselle's voice rose above the sound of my body being shattered, the grunts of air as they escaped me. I could do nothing to stop the slide of my body down the wall, barely catching myself with my left arm. The right was shattered at the elbow; I barely remembered it happening. What shocked me was the fact that they stopped at Giselle's command,

and then the pain rolled over me, and for a moment I blacked out.

As I came to, voices floated around me.

"You have been misled. As have we. I see that she even left a stunt double."

Daughter of a whore, did that mean that Milly wasn't here? A part of me was glad, and the other part was just fucking pissed.

"She said you'd claim that."

"Convenient," Giselle said, her voice dry. There was the rustle of someone's clothes, then, "The least you could do is ease her pain since you attacked us first. You do have the proper herbs, don't you?"

There was a sputter of disbelief, and then a pair of hands went around my neck. I opened my eyes to look up into the face of a freaking angel. She was stunning, the lines of her face reminiscent of the classic beauties, feminine and soft, full lips, huge blue-green eyes framed with dark lashes and a button nose.

Her voice was high-pitched, yet easy on the ears. "Milly told us you could hold back your Immunity on your hands? Do it and I will heal you."

Giselle came into my line of sight and gave me a nod. She thought it was a good idea, though I wasn't so sure. With an effort, I peeled my Immunity back, my fingers bared to whatever magic the witch would use on me.

Her fingers touched mine. "Hold still, this will hurt, but it will be quick and your body will be whole."

A soft tingle was the first of it, and then my broken bones did a jig, yanking back into place. I bit my tongue on the scream that rose up, shaking as my body re-knit itself. I was shocked—and not just at the pain.

Milly had always claimed that healing like this wasn't possible. That it wasn't *just* not one of her talents, but that you couldn't heal people with magic.

Fool me once, shame on you. Fool me twice, shame on me. Fool me a third time, and I'm going to run you the fuck through.

Panting, I lay still while my body finished mending itself under the guidance of the witch's magic. The pain slowly lessened and the click of bone snapping back together slowed until there was nothing but the beat of my heart in my ears.

I pushed myself into a sitting position, my back against the wall, one sword across my lap the other on the floor beside me.

"Cannonballs. Nasty, but effective," I said, pushing one of the iron balls with my left foot.

The man I'd stabbed sat up from across the room, the healer stepping away from him. The woman whose arm I'd removed was not in the room. How long had I been out for? "We thought it pertinent, considering your innate ability to avoid magic, to be prepared for an attack."

A snort escaped me. "Attack? I'm not here for you. I'm here for Milly."

The witches stilled around us. Apparently, honesty is not always the best policy.

Giselle stepped between us, as if her frail body could withstand even one blow from a cannonball. "Milly has betrayed not only us, but your Coven as well."

The woman, the one who'd healed me, held her hand up for silence. "The rest of you may stay, but I will lead this. I knew Milly the best. She was like my sister."

My stomach felt as if it had been yanked out and dropped from the window, the words striking me as easily as one of those gods-be-damned cannonballs. This woman was like Milly's sister? Then what the hell was I? And why did I care?

I was a goddamned fucking idiot. That was what I was.

Giselle turned her face away, shaking her head. Tears slipped down her cheeks, and I knew that we'd both been fooled. We had been completely blinded by our love for Milly. She'd been able to manipulate us into believing her, and worse, trusting her.

I pushed myself to my feet and with great care cleaned off my one blade, before sliding it into its sheath. With my foot, I flicked the second blade up into the air and put it away too. "Let me guess," I said. "Milly told you something along the lines of Giselle and I had her under our control, and she needed you to watch out for her. Help her train so she could eventually escape? Some shit like that?"

The members of the Coven exchanged glances. Even if I wasn't bang on, I was close enough.

Laughing, I touched one finger to my chin. "Would you like to know what she told us about you? The Coven is ignorant of the world and you demanded her complete devotion; you forced her to cut ties with us and the world. And in the end, you wanted to kill her."

The witch with the angelic good looks seemed shocked, her hand going to her throat. "We would never ask her to cut ties with her family. It is a support system that every witch needs. I can't believe Milly would tell you that . . . no, you must have been mistaken." She lifted her hands and three of the cannonballs rose in the air. Ah, crap, I did not want to get smashed again.

Giselle put her hands on her hips. "There was a witch who'd gone with Milly on the last salvage. She was the Coven leader's wife?"

Eyes widened throughout the room. "Why would you say that?"

My mentor closed her eyes, and I felt her draw on her abilities. I wanted to stop her, to stay her hand and keep her sanity with us a little longer. "Milly was having an affair with the Coven leader. What better way to remove the wife from the picture than to have a Tracker kill her rival in self-defense?"

Now, I won't say I'd forgotten about killing that particular witch, it just didn't make me lose any sleep. She'd been about to kill Milly, and at the time, I couldn't let that happen.

Three of the witches turned to face the one man I'd laid my blade on, the blond. He went deathly pale as he addressed the angelic witch. "It is why I stepped down, Terese. I knew I was wrong and was using my connections for Milly. But I did love her."

"Past tense?" I asked.

His shoulders tightened up, almost imperceptibly, then slowly relaxed. "Past tense. She asked of me things I could not do. Spells she wanted that I was unwilling to give her. For all her strength, and she is the strongest to wield wild magic in centuries, there is a darkness in her." He scrubbed a hand through his hair. "It was too late when I saw it, too late to stop her."

Terese was shaking her head. "No, I won't believe it!"

I'd had enough of this diplomacy crap. Two strides and I was in Terese's face, not even an inch away. "She's trying to kill my family, has spelled an anklet that drains the wearer's life away, has threatened the life of my werewolf—"

Stunned silence met my words and they exchanged glances several times before anyone spoke.

"Did you say your werewolf?" Terese asked, her brows knitting over her ridiculously stunning eyes.

"Um, yeah." I wasn't sure what I'd stepped in now.

Terese pursed her lips. "Would you be willing to have us lay a truth spell on you?"

"It won't work, but sure," I said, wanting to hurry this up.

"Then we'll lay it on her." Terese pointed at Giselle, who nodded without hesitation.

"I will, if you will answer questions for us, and if once you see the truth, you will make a peace pact with Rylee."

Terese agreed and the others stepped around us in a circle. My shoulders tightened with anticipation; I didn't like people where I couldn't see them.

The thing was, I wasn't sure what a truth spell entailed, and I should have known better than to just agree. Should have, but I thought Giselle knew what she was up to. Of course, that was just it, she did.

Terese beckoned to Giselle to kneel in front of her, and then placed one hand on either side of her head.

"*En memories benefactor justifus.*" Terese intoned.

Giselle flexed and let out a moan. Terese's eyes glazed over and I realized that she was seeing what Giselle had seen as she flinched and her face grew sorrowful. Tears slipped down her creamy skin, and I hated her a little. Terese had no right to be upset; Milly had been my best friend, not hers. And no, I don't care how stupid that sounds.

Terese let go of Giselle. "They are speaking the truth. I have seen it. Milly is not who we thought she was." She covered her lips with her dainty freaking fingers. The murmuring started and she lifted a hand again for silence. "We must meet with the full Coven. There are things Milly has done that you could not know were against our precepts."

"You mean like the anklet?" I asked.

Terese nodded. "The threat to your wolf, that alone will gain her excommunication."

That surprised me. "Why?"

"The local pack is a part of our extended family, if you will. Milly was their liaison." Terese stared at me, as if willing me to understand the unspoken words.

It only took me about two seconds to put it together. Milly was in good with the pack, and the pack was trying to kill Alex. I thought back to when the pack had chased us and Milly had refused to do anything about it. All the puzzle pieces were becoming painfully, razor-sharp clear.

The rage that had dimmed with the pummeling I'd taken came flooding back, my muscles awash with adrenaline. I stood there, shaking, but unable to move just yet.

"Then you have no problem if I kill her?" I asked, proud at how steady my voice was, how quiet and deadly.

Terese stared at me, the pulse in her throat jumping. "I saw her connection to you through your mentor's eyes. If you must kill her, there will be no retribution from us."

The other witches gasped and the previous Coven leader, Milly's boy-toy, stepped forward, mouth a thin line, eyes hard with anger.

"No, Milly could be helped—"

This time it was Giselle who lifted her hand in a sharp slashing movement, cutting him off.

"No, she can't. The darkness in her has taken root; the only way to keep that darkness from spreading is to destroy its vessel."

Her words hung in the air, and the finality of the situation slid over me. Milly—for all the love I'd had for her, for the memories we shared, the oaths we'd taken together—would never be back.

This was it.

I was going to kill my best friend.

6

The first thing Terese did was make a blood oath with me, one of peace. One that would keep me on the good side of the Coven, regardless of the fact that I was going to kill Milly.

We repeated the necessary words as blood from a finger prick from each of us dropped into an open brazier.

"By blood and oath, a binding tie between magic, death, and honor."

Thank the gods it was simple and no freaking Latin.

Terese sent us off with a pre-made spell that would enclose Milly and put her to sleep, making the final blow easier on both of us. Of course, after Terese had told us everything Milly had been telling the Coven, I wasn't so sure I wanted to go easy on my former best friend.

"We know all your secrets, Rylee—about your Immunity and the best way to work around it. About your Tracking and the ways she'd learnt to shift someone's threads and the vibrations they gave off to another. She knows your strengths and your weaknesses, and will use them against you, as she did us. My only piece of advice is to kill her swiftly."

What had infuriated me the most was, as we drove away, knowing I had to leave for London and wouldn't be able to take care of Milly until I got back. She was a burr under my skin, itching and irritating the hell out of me. How was I going to find the witch if I couldn't Track her? Shit, I'd have never thought someone could shift vibrations; the threads always seemed so distinct to me.

Was that what had happened with my last salvage and the trolls? Maybe that hadn't been troll magic shifting the kid's energies, masking them so I thought he was still alive.

Fuck, maybe it had been Milly.

More than ever, I knew I needed to get to London and learn from the Tracker waiting there. I had to believe that Jack Feen would have the answers.

I turned my head to look at Giselle. Her eyes were closed and she was leaning back in the seat.

"Giselle," I said softly. "Are you okay?"

"Just tired. A truth spell is one that drains the person it's used on."

"Do you want me to pull over, or . . ." Damn, I didn't know what she would need. I'd never had a spell used on me and never would; I had no idea what would help the recovery time.

"No, just take us home. That is where I need to be."

I drove as fast as I dared on the winter-kissed roads. Black ice was a bitch, and I'd already had one accident that winter. I had no need to make it a repeat event.

We pulled into the driveway and made it all the way up to the farmhouse before I registered that Giselle had gone very still. I slammed the Jeep into park and reached over, putting my fingers against her throat.

My own heart hammered so hard I wasn't sure what I was feeling, if anything.

"Giselle, please, not yet."

I pressed harder up under her jaw. Almost ten seconds passed before the flutter of a heartbeat brushed against my fingertips, like the touch of a butterfly's wing, it was so hesitant.

Leaping out of the Jeep, I ran around to the passenger side and opened the door. *This couldn't be it, it just couldn't.* With as much care as I had in me, I lifted Giselle out and half-jogged, half-speed walked up to the house, somehow managing to open the door without putting her down.

Placing Giselle in my bed, I again felt for a heartbeat. The feel of her blood pumping was faint, and so subtle, so quiet I could hardly convince myself that she was in fact still alive.

She let out a moan and I sat beside her. "Giselle, what do you need?"

Her eyes fluttered and opened, staring up at me. "It is time, my girl."

My heart slammed against my chest. "No, not yet." I reached out and touched the side of her face, feeling the coolness of her skin. I pulled the blankets around her, and then curled up beside her, giving her the warmth of my own body. Her hand lifted in the air, then dropped light as a feather onto my hip.

"I've told you much, but there is a little more." She took a breath, but her chest didn't rise, as if the air were escaping her somehow.

I closed my eyes and put my face into the crook of her neck, breathed in deep, as if I could somehow help her. I could say nothing, didn't trust my voice to do anything but crack and crumble under the strain of my heart breaking.

"You will need this." She touched the opal stone hanging from her neck. "I cannot see clearly why, only that you must take it with you to London."

I put my hand over hers. "All right."

Her eyelids fluttered and her body shivered. I held her tighter, as if I could stop her from going. Even I couldn't stop death, though, no matter my abilities.

"You are more than a Tracker, Rylee, and in some ways, that is the least of your worries." She took a breath, let it out, took another. "You are touched with the Blood of the Lost."

I circled her with my arms, not caring what she said, only knowing that it would be the last I ever heard her speak. Let her tell me to find my blue socks for years, I would take that over this. But it wasn't my choice, and in my heart I knew that she wanted to be free of the madness.

"Rylee."

The thrum of her heart, unsteady and hesitant as if it wasn't sure it would give another beat, thumped pitifully against my ear.

"I'm here," I said, my voice thick with unshed tears.

"My last advice for you." She paused, her opposite hand coming across to stroke my face as she spoke. "Trust your heart, always. Even when your head tells you not to, it is your strength. And remember that I love you—" Giselle took a sharp shuddering breath and I froze, my mind and heart screaming together a cacophony of denial.

"Giselle?" I sat up and her hand slid off my hip, limply falling onto the bed. I stared down at her and knew without Tracking her that she was gone, but I did it anyway, reaching out in desperation for her threads.

They gave off the dim glow of the newly deceased, and I stumbled backwards, tripping over my own feet in an effort to get away.

She was the last of my family, the whole reason I was able to face the world and make the tough decisions. Because I knew she was with me, she was the one who'd helped me heal after my adoptive parents turned their backs on me. Giselle was the one who'd shown me it was safe to love someone.

I found my way to the living room and fell to my knees in front of the big bay window. In my mind's eye, I could see Giselle and Alex sitting in front of me, looking out the window, their heads bowed together. Closing my eyes, I leaned forward until my head touched the wooden floors. This was not happening. So fast, so unexpected, I couldn't make heads or tails of what to do next. I stayed there, breathed in the scent of old wood and lemons from the polish, and let my mind go blank. Let myself forget what had happened.

My old rotary phone rang, snapping my head up off the floor. I fought off the rush of blood and wondered distantly how long I'd been kneeling—my sense of time distorted with my grief. I forced myself to my feet and walked, albeit somewhat unsteadily, into the kitchen to pick up the phone, my body and mind in complete disconnect.

"Hello?"

A young girl spoke on the other end, and it took me a minute to recognize her. India, the child I'd rescued with O'Shea; a girl with talents that were even now growing and changing.

"Rylee, Giselle says you don't have time to grieve. You have to go after the kids in London and then kick Milly's" —her voice dropped to a whisper— "ass. I've got to go now, my mom is coming."

The phone call ended with a click and I stared down at it.

"Still bossing me around," I said, a pitiful attempt at a laugh escaping my lips. "Okay, I've got it. Kids first, Milly second, grieve third."

I made a phone call to Agent Valley. He didn't answer, so I left him a message. There was no need for a care aide for Giselle now.

Alex came trotting into the kitchen from outside as I hung up the phone for the second time, his coat dusted in snow, his tongue lolling out. "Hey ho. Rylee play?"

"No, not right now."

He cocked his head to one side. "Giselle play?"

My throat tightened and I shook my head. "No. Giselle died."

Alex's eyes widened and he sat back on his haunches, his big paws slapping over his elongated muzzle. "No, no, no. Alex love Giselle. Giselle not dead!" He let out a howl, the sound ripping though the house, tearing through me and heightening my own sorrow.

I wished that I could howl with him, let my grief fling far and wide until I was wrung out, but that was a luxury I could not afford. Not yet anyway.

I dropped to my knees in front of the werewolf and wrapped my arms around him. "I loved her too, but right now we need to be strong. Giselle wants us to go find those kids in London."

Alex sniffled and whimpered, continuing to whisper, "no, no, no." As if he could somehow take away her death. I clung to him, my last tie to a family I'd put together in bits and pieces.

Closing my eyes, I tried to imagine how the hell my life would go without Giselle in it.

And for the life of me, I couldn't see anything but an empty hole.

7

Sweat pooled on my lower back, the plush seat wrapping me like a stifling hug from an overbearing aunt. Fumbling at the seatbelt, I stood up and walked to the thick black line I wasn't to cross, and then back to my seat in an attempt to calm down. The Boeing 747 was huge, especially since it wasn't set to be a typical commercial craft. The back half where I was sectioned off was open, more like a living room than an airplane.

Even though Agent Valley assured me that the FBI had rigged this plane to be impervious to the vibrations supernaturals gave off, I still wasn't allowed any closer than necessary to the engines and the navigational equipment. Hence the thick black line on the cream colored carpeting.

Smart, but it made me wonder just *how* safe their crappy plane actually was. I paced my small area, the circle of my steps tightening with each round until I was back at my seat.

Eve had offered to fly to London, but I'd turned her down. Since it would take her at least a week, hopping from island to island across the Pacific Ocean then flying up the coast of Africa, or even if she went up the east coast through Canada and across Greenland I told her to go back to Eagle and her training. The reality was if she couldn't come with us, by the time she got to London, everything would be done. Alex and I would be on our own on this run. My mind shifted to Giselle and my heart clenched with sorrow.

Not yet.

Though Eve had argued half-heartedly, I could see by the glimmer in her eyes she was excited to go back to the Guardian and his training with her.

Alex hadn't moved from his spot beside me, his claws carefully lifting the shade on the window up and down, like he was hypnotized. Which was not a bad thing after waking up to him howling Giselle's name every hour the night before.

I leaned back in the chair and scrubbed at my over-tired eyes, listening to the voices floating back to me. I couldn't hear what they were saying.

Hmm. But Alex could.

I tapped him on the shoulder and he rolled his head upside down to look at me. "Alex, what are they saying?" I pointed to the front of the plane.

He tipped his head, then lifted one floppy ear with the tips of two claws to hear better.

I had to smother a laugh, and once more, I was grateful he was with me.

"Parachutes. And plane crash," he said, tongue flicking out to dangle in front of his nose.

My gut tightened and I no longer thought this trip was a good idea. Another Tracker or not, if I died on this flight because of whatever vibrations Alex and I gave off . . . who the hell knew if Agent Valley was even telling the truth? He could just be making things up as he went in order to get me to agree.

The engines rumbled and the plane started to move. Shit, too late to change my mind now.

I snapped my seatbelt on and then wrestled with Alex to do the same for him. Pouting, he sat awkwardly in the seat made for people, legs sticking out, arms folded across his chest. His body just didn't quite work with the seat, but at least he was strapped in.

The flight attendant, Agent Valley, and another agent I didn't recognize except for the standard FBI suit and tie, made their way to their seats and buckled up. A fourth person who had on a deep red hoodie, which covered his face, slipped into the seat at the very front, farthest away from me and Alex. Agent Valley called over his shoulder to me.

"This is your first time flying, isn't it?"

I thought about Eve and me flying high over New Mexico. So maybe this wasn't the same thing, but riding a Harpy with no rigging to hold you on was no mean feat.

"Nah."

"Excellent. Then we won't have to sedate you."

Laughter followed his comment, and I grit my teeth. They must have seen me pacing. Assholes.

"Good thing you won't have to try," I said. "I'd hate to see your nose broken again, though I doubt it could look much worse than it does now."

A sharp intake of air from the other agent and a muffled laugh from the guy in the hoodie filtered back to me. I settled back into my seat and closed my eyes. I could do this, I would not freak out, I would not freak out, I would not freak out . . . .

As the plane pulled into the air, my stomach dropped and I couldn't stop myself from clenching the armrests. A distraction, that was what I needed. I pulled the opal pendant out of my left pocket and dangled it in front of me. No need to wear it, but I was going to keep it close. Giselle had never been wrong about her predictions, so I knew that at some point there would be a use for it. It spun slowly in the air, little pricks of color sparkled, and I mulled over the possibilities. Maybe I'd be dealing with another Reader, someone I would need to be lucid in order to crack the case.

"Alex sick."

My eyes darted sideways to see Alex with his tongue hanging out, saliva pouring off it like a miniature river. Oh, shit, this was not good. I jammed the pendant back in my pocket, unbuckled him and clenched my hand around his collar, dragging him toward the bathroom as the plane climbed.

"Ma'am, you can't leave your seat!" The flight attendant shouted at me.

"You do not want him puking anywhere but in the toilet!" I shouted back, thinking of all the food he'd eaten that morning.

We barely made it to the closet of a bathroom before Alex heaved his guts out, just making it into the tiny toilet. How people ever thought the mile high club was a good idea, I couldn't see. We barely fit and we'd left the door open.

Alex retched until there was nothing left, which looked to be about four pounds of breakfast and snacks. Nothing that would have stayed in a barf bag, that was for sure.

I filled the sink with water and, taking a cloth, wiped his muzzle and face down. "Feel better now?"

He bobbed his head. "Tired."

Slowly, Alex weaving like a drunk, we made our way back to our seats. The plane leveled off and the flight attendant came around. I took a ginger ale for Alex and a bottle of water for me.

To be in a place where the people didn't freak out about Alex handling the pop can in an almost human manner, his claws gripping the condensation covered sides, was to say the least, strange.

Of course, he was also wearing his collar so maybe they were just seeing a large, and extremely dexterous, dog. Drinking pop.

I took a sip of my water and leaned my head back. I had a feeling it was going to be a long flight, and I prayed it wouldn't continue as it had begun.

The smell of blood and flesh filled his nostrils. Tipping his head back, he breathed deeply, the fresh snow almost burying the trail he'd been following. A nearly inaudible crack of a twig underfoot brought his ears swiveling around, listening for the game he'd been trailing.

The flash of tan and a flick of a white tail as the deer caught his scent launched him into action.

Chasing the deer, lusting after the warm juices that would flow once he brought it down, it was easy to forget that he wasn't just a wolf. That he was also a man. A man who'd left his world behind for this one. His thoughts betrayed him and his footsteps faltered, giving the deer the chance it needed to escape.

Unable to control himself, he shifted into his two-legged form, the sudden change in perspective throwing him off balance. As naked as the day he was born, he wobbled, and then fell to one knee.

The cold winter air bit along his bare skin, but he took it in, appreciated that he could feel it. The first few weeks of being a shifter, he'd taken out his rage on the local pack. They'd quickly realized he wasn't to be ignored, and when he staked his claim around Rylee's property, they'd backed off. Now though, he had no purpose. And still, he couldn't bring himself to go back to the world that had once been the only one he'd known. The thing was, he wasn't just a wolf. Something else lurked inside of him.

"What am I doing?" His voice hoarse from disuse.

A feminine sultry voice whispered across his skin, like fingers trailing along the overheated flesh. "Running away. That's what you're doing. But you don't have to run, Liam."

He spun in the snow, half-crouched, a snarl on his lips.

Dressed all in white, down to a thick white wolf pelt for a jacket and white boots topped with rabbit fur, Milly watched him with her bright green eyes. He resisted the urge to cover himself, but stayed in a crouch effectively blocking her roving, hungry eyes.

"How . . ." he coughed, clearing his throat. "Did you find me?"

She smiled and actually batted her eyelashes at him, as if that would work. "A friend of mine has a special place in his heart for wolves. A connection, if you will. He sent me to find you. To help you."

O'Shea took a deep breath and caught the scent of another wolf. Narrowing his eyes, he let out a low growl. A flicker or movement twenty feet or so behind Milly confirmed his nose. She'd used a wolf to find him, to track his scent. But the wolf was a submissive, he could smell that much, and it was enough for him to dismiss the other shifter.

Did he trust her? O'Shea wasn't sure. Rylee had trusted her, but did she still?

Taking the better, smarter path, he kept his mouth shut.

Milly filled in the silence. "I have something for you, something that will help you be human. You can chase the wolf back with it. Permanently."

Lifting her hand, she dangled a woven strand of metal that, by the smell of it, was gold and diamonds. A torc, made to slip over his neck.

"You could keep her safe if you could control your wolf. As an Alpha, it can take years to gain the control you need. She could die in that time. But with this you could keep her safe."

His insides twisted at the thought of hurting Rylee, his desire to protect her overriding whatever other sense he might have at the moment. If it weren't for the rage that took him unawares, he would have sought Rylee out already. As it was, he couldn't trust himself not to kill her. A part of him knew that it wasn't just the wolf that made him this way; it was something else. Something stronger.

Milly took a few steps closer, holding the torc out. "You don't have to fight the beast in you if you don't want to."

The wolf inside of him spoke softly, though it was images more than words. *I am a part of you now. Together we are strong. Alone, we are weak.*

The wolf was right, and though a part of him wanted to silence the rage, he knew he had to figure this out on his own. Even if it did take years.

Stepping back, he shook his head. "No, I have to find the balance. Thank you, Milly." He turned his back to her and let the shift begin to take him.

"I'm sorry you feel that way, Liam," she said softly, the scent of ozone snapping through the air. "Truly, I am sorry."

With the suddenness that only nature can provide, lightning cracked through the air, slamming into O'Shea's body, stopping his shift. Light and dark danced in his vision, eyes of green coming into sharp focus as Milly bent over him.

The cold metal torc slid around his neck, tightening like the collar it was.

"Come now," Milly said softly, drawing him to his feet, his mind screaming that he couldn't go with her, that she was one of the ones, obvious now, that would hurt Rylee. But his body wouldn't respond, bound tight by the spelled torc hanging so innocently around his neck.

With a smile that turned down at the edges, liquid brimming in her eyes, Milly brushed back a lock of his hair. "You have much to learn, Liam. So much to learn."

We were somewhere over the Atlantic when Agent Valley finally deemed me worth coming to speak to rather than just shouting at me from across the plane. Apparently, he was still stinging from our encounter at my house. Too damn bad. I wasn't here to pander to his emotional issues. Bad enough that I struggled to deal with my own and Alex's.

Standing next to me, he held out a yellow manila envelope. "Here are some of the pictures of the children who've been taken. Now that you're on the case, you can start Tracking them." He flopped the envelope into my lap and walked back to his seat. Yup, definitely still pissy.

Sliding the pictures out, I cradled them in my lap. Each one had a name printed neatly on the back. I looked for Sophia's, as she was the first to go missing, and according to Valley, wouldn't stand a chance of being alive.

I reached out for her, to Track her, and encountered a big fat nothing. My muscles clenched and Alex turned to me as my heart rate spiked. No, this couldn't be happening, not now, not again.

Only one other child had ever proved impossible for me to Track. My sister, Berget. When she went missing, my Tracker abilities came online, only I didn't know that until later. Every attempt I'd ever made to Track her once I knew what I was doing, to bring her body home so that she could be at peace finally, had ended in exactly this same feeling. Nothing.

Even if the child was dead, I should still be able to find them; I could still Track them. But this emptiness, this impossible feeling that they never even existed? Shit on a stick, I was in trouble. Trembling, I pulled another picture out, Benjamin, and Tracked his threads, looking where they should have been.

And got the same damn result. Nothing, a big fat emptiness in my head where the traces of his life should have been.

Shit, shit, shit.

I went through the whole pile of pictures and couldn't get a bead on a single one of the kids. What the hell was I going to do if I couldn't Track? Tucking the pictures back into the envelope, I stood and headed to the bathroom.

Locking the door behind me, I leaned on the sink, attempted to slow my breathing and heart down. This wasn't possible. I'd never had this problem before except with Berget. But she was an anomaly. Even Giselle, when she'd still been lucid, had thought that Berget was a one-off, a single case that I would likely never have to deal with again. And now I had twenty-plus kids falling into the same category as Berget. What the fuck was I going to do?

The mirror reflected my eyes back to me, wide and sketchy, the tri-colored rings swirling with gold, green, and dark brown. My skin was pale and I leaned forward, not wanting to see the evidence of my imminent failure. The minute we landed, I'd be screwed.

How did I tell them that I couldn't sense the kids? What would I do with my life if I couldn't Track?

I splashed water over my face and put a cold, wet paper towel over the back of my neck. A soft knock on the door barely made me twitch.

"Ma'am," the flight attendant said, her voice sharp like she was hoping something was wrong with me. "Are you alright in there?"

"I'm fine. Fuck off," I barked. I heard Alex repeat the 'fuck off' and the flight attendant gasped; then it went quiet outside the door.

I tried again to Track the kids, going through their names one by one, hoping by all that was holy in this world that it was a glitch, some sort of freaky accident that was done and gone.

Nope, still nothing.

Wracking my brain, I wished that I could phone Giselle when we landed, and ask her to help me through this. Bile rose in the back of my throat, coating my tongue. Between the grief of losing my mentor, and the fear of what was happening. I could barely breathe.

It took everything I had to still my mind and look at this in a more logical way.

I was going to see another Tracker—he would help me. Jack Feen would know what was going on. He had to. Clinging to the faint hope that a man I'd never met would be able to solve a riddle I didn't understand, I left the privacy of the bathroom and went back to my seat.

I didn't look at the pictures again, couldn't. Because if I no longer had the ability to Track, I had no idea what I would do with my life.

From my seat, I listened to the conversations around me, an attempt to subdue the panic in my heart futile. Until I heard a voice I recognized. The kid in the red hoodie, the one who'd come in last and slumped down into his seat. Agent Valley was just leaving him and heading back to his own seat.

Kyle, that little bastard was on the plane? Here was the distraction I needed.

Jerking to my feet, I stumbled all the way to the black line, hesitated, and then strode over it. Agent Valley and his partner threw themselves at me, and with a roundhouse and two swift front kicks, I dropped them one right after the other. Hunched in his seat, Kyle seemed oblivious to what was going on. The agents were pulling themselves to their feet, and the flight attendant was standing against the far aisle, her eyes bugging out, her hands twitching.

Kyle's hoodie was down, and his ears were plugged with headphones. Perfect, he never even saw me coming, the cocky little shit.

I reached down and clamped a hand over his shoulder, digging my nails into his scrawny frame. Letting out a yelp, he looked up and paled. I dragged him out of his seat and back to my area of the plane while he begged and pleaded.

"Rylee, I'm sorry, I just couldn't keep something like this a secret! A huge government cover-up! Please, listen to me, I didn't mean to get you in trouble. I wouldn't have come to your place or taken the papers, but I couldn't get back into the FBI files, they blocked me after I hacked in . . . you had the only proof that the government knew about supernatural beings—"

"Shut the fuck up," I said as I reached the black line and tossed him over it.

He scrambled backwards until he was pressed against the far wall, sweat beading up on his forehead.

"Please don't kill me." He whimpered, a tear trickling out the corner of one eye.

What an idiot. "I'm not going to kill you."

"You aren't?"

"No, but I'm going to make sure you never do anything so goddamn stupid again."

The throb of his Adam's apple as he attempted to swallow was almost comical. More than that, he was giving me an outlet for my own fears. Sure, it wasn't fair, but the kid deserved at least an ass-kicking for double-crossing me. If he'd been an adult, it would not have gone so easy for him.

The two agents nearly tumbled over themselves in order to place their bodies between me and Kyle.

"I'm not going to kill him," I said, one hand resting on my hip. "The shit had the nerve to play me. I can't let that go. You know what that would do to my reputation?" I was completely making this part up. I had no idea if I even *had* a reputation, nor cared if it was affected in any way if I did have one. However, they didn't know that.

Agent Valley cleared his throat. "And what do you have in mind for him?"

"Well, he works for you now, doesn't he?"

The FBI agent nodded once. "Yes, he is far too talented to be left out on his own. We might as well make use of his particular talents."

I smiled; Agent Valley's eyes narrowed. "Yeah, I'm thinking I will make good use of his talents too. For free, for the rest of his ever-loving life. Got it? He will be my personal hacker in everything I do; he will work for me pro bono until I deem he's worked off his debt, if that time ever comes."

Kyle scrambled forward on his knees. "I can do that. I can."

Agent Valley's eyes narrowed further, to mere slits. "You aren't going to hurt him?"

Again, I smiled. "Oh, I never said that. I just said I wouldn't kill him."

8

My fingers gripped Alex's collar as we stood in the pouring rain arguing with Agent Valley. Kyle slinked off with the other agent, still rubbing his ass from the full on over-my-knee spanking I'd given him with the flat of my sword. That made me smile. He wanted to act like an idiot child, so I'd treated him like one.

"I want to meet the Tracker first. I'm not going to the police station until I meet him." I had to dig my heels in on this—there was no other way. I had to figure out what was stopping me from Tracking these kids. Had I lost my ability somehow? I harbored a fear that this sudden change had to do with the demon venom I'd carried around last month. Shit, as if almost dying wasn't enough, the venom had to leave me useless too?

Alex picked up on my tension and let out a whimper, but said nothing. I'd told him that he couldn't speak a word while we were in London unless there was no one else around. So far, he was remembering.

"Ms. Adamson," Agent Valley said. "Our number one priority should be the children, shouldn't it?"

Guilt tactics, fuck I hated them. I used them on myself enough. I didn't need the agent piling on the weight.

Time to get seriously tough. "They're dead. Correct?"

He flinched as if I'd hit him. "Yes." He was going to have to learn how to hide his 'tells.' Already, I was gaining the upper hand; something I'd never managed with O'Shea.

"Then they won't mind waiting another couple of hours."

With that argument, I won out and was taken to the hospital where Jack Feen was slowly dying. We pulled up and I stared out at the tall, greyish concrete building, the exterior as depressing as no doubt the interior was with all the sickness and death hidden behind the walls.

I leashed Alex, and tugged him tight against my leg. This was the first time I'd taken him to a hospital and I was worried he might be overwhelmed, not only by the smells, but the strong emotions. As I'd learned last month, the werewolf was sensitive to the emotions other people threw off. Which was not necessarily a good thing.

But Alex tucked in against my left leg, heeling at my side like a well-trained mutt. Which is all the humans would see, as long as his spelled collar stayed on.

I turned and looked down into the car. "Aren't you coming in?"

Agent Valley shook his head. "No, I will be heading to the local station. I'll send a car round for you. You have one hour, Ms. Adamson."

Giving him a sloppy salute and swirling my wrist like a girly girl, I spun on one boot heel and walked away. Alex snickered under his breath. "Funny Rylee."

"No talking," I said, though my voice was far from harsh. Even with the fear of losing my Tracking ability, even with the loss of Giselle so sharp, I was excited. I was about to meet someone who knew what the hell he was doing, and he could share that knowledge with me.

We stopped at the front desk, I gave told them Alex was a therapy dog, and got directions to Jack Feen's room. He was on the fifth floor. Alex and I took the stairs. Elevators mostly worked for me, but with Alex too, it might be too much for the technology to handle. Today was not a day I wanted to get stuck in an elevator.

I thought about what Agent Valley had told me on the plane, explaining the science behind the truths I'd lived for most of my life.

"We've found a very specific vibration that supernaturals give off, almost like their own EMP pulse, though with some subtle differences. You each have a radius, and the more supernaturals, the larger the radius of technology that is affected. There are a few things that can protect equipment, iron plating coated with a skin of silver is the best."

I'd stared at him somewhat blankly. They were studying supernaturals? Though I supposed I shouldn't have been surprised, it unnerved me. The more the FBI learned about us, the easier we would be to corral. Control. Not what I had in mind. So I asked questions.

"So why don't guns work?"

Agent Valley tapped one tooth with his index finger before answering. "The best way to explain it is that everything has positive and negative vibrations of energy."

My eyes widened. Crap, this sounded like he'd actually done some research and believed what he'd found.

"And the primer in explosives of all types has a, more or less, negative energy."

"That's not surprising," I said.

He grunted and kept going.

"Most supernaturals have a positive type energy that they throw off. When the two come into contact, the positive energy does, for lack of a better explanation, weird shit. It's why bullets swerve, guns misfire, and occasionally everything works fine. It's literally a crap shoot."

Well, that explained a number of things I'd always just taken on faith. Don't play with guns and don't touch technology. That shit will break on your ass when you need it the most.

Blinking, I looked up at the door I stood in front of. 'Jack Feen' was etched into a small nameplate. Somehow, I didn't think it was a good thing that he had his own plaque.

Glancing back the way we'd come, I saw a nurse wave at me from the desk. I gave her a bob of my head in acknowledgment.

Lifting my hand, I knocked on the door.

"Come the bloody fucking hell in or bloody fuck the hell off! But don't just stand out there hovering in front of my fucking goddamned door!"

Swallowing hard, I pushed the door open. Alex and I stepped into the room. The air was cold, the window halfway open and the winter wind whipping through. Pale yellow walls that were meant to be cheery only made me think that the shade had been handpicked for Jack. His skin was the same pale tone, and contrasted sharply with his bright red hair. Not a good look. There was no IV or other instrument connected to him—of course, to get them to work would be a freaking miracle. He was here to die, slowly, and by the looks of the bare surfaces around him, alone. No flowers, no balloons, not even a single get well card. I drew closer to the bed, Alex trying to hide behind me and tangling my legs.

"Alex," I grunted, grabbing at the bed to stop my downward tumble.

"What the fuck? You brought a fucking goddamn werewolf into a bloody hospital? Woman, are you out of your ever-fucking mind?"

Damn, and I thought I had a potty mouth.

"He's fine. Just klutzy." I stared down at the Tracker, at a loss for words.

"Well? What are you here for? Charity? Motherfuckers don't realize I ain't got no fucking money left. Sons of bitches have bled me dry." He let out a wheezing laugh that ended in a rattling cough.

I pulled a chair up, and took a closer look at his face as I spoke. "My name is Rylee, and I'm a Tracker."

This close I could see that he didn't have *just* blue eyes. They swirled with three shades, light almost grey-blue, a dark blue the color of a lapis stone, and a bright blue like a summer sky. At least I knew now why my eyes were the way they were. Looked like it was an outward sign of a Tracker.

"Tracker, eh? That what you think?"

"It's why I'm here. To finish the job you started."

He pursed his lips, eyes narrowing to mere slits. Had I pissed him off? With me, that was a definite possibility.

"You know what you're doing?" He asked. "Who trained you? Brin has been dead for years and he was the last Tracker on your side of the water by your accent."

Excitement coursed through me and I tucked the name away. Brin. I would look him up when I got home—better yet, I'd have Kyle do it. "My mentor was Giselle, but she wasn't a Tracker. I was hoping you'd tell me what you know."

His eye snapped wide. "No one trained you?"

I shook my head, my one hand resting on Alex's back as he sniffed at the edges of the bed.

"Well, fuck. How the hell didn't you kill yourself?"

"Ah . . ."

"Never mind. Come here, let me have a look at you." He beckoned with a gnarled up hand, the skin drawn tight over the bones to the point that I could actually see the blood pulse through his veins. Crap, this was like some creepy-ass freak show.

I scooted my chair forward and he took my hand gently, which surprised the hell out of me. "What can you do besides Tracking?"

He turned my hand over and I answered. "I'm an Immune."

Chuckling, he nodded. "I wondered when I couldn't get a bead on you. I'm a Reader."

I nodded, recognizing the name as one of many Giselle went by. Looked like he'd dodged the curse that had claimed her. I'd say he was lucky, but by the looks of things now, maybe not so much.

"Do all Trackers have multiple abilities?"

Holding my hand lightly, he touched a scar above my wrist. "Yes. It's necessary in order to be a good Tracker to have some additional abilities. It seems the gods favored us and cursed us all in one breath."

Alex lifted his head up and peeked over the edge of the bed at Jack, his claws curling around the bunched up blankets.

He took a sniff and wrinkled his nose. "Sick?"

Jack looked down at the werewolf. "Dying."

With an exaggerated pout, Alex flopped onto his ass. "Alex no like dying. Dying sucks shit."

A burst of laughter escaped Jack. "Yeah, that's what I think too." His eyes flicked up to mine. "Comic relief, I like it. Keep him close; you'll need all the laughs you can get. The longer you're in this business, the less you'll feel like smiling."

The smile that had teased at the edges of my mouth slipped. "Jack, what can you tell me about being a Tracker? I feel like I won't get another chance like this . . ." I trailed off, not wanting to point out the obvious.

Shifting his weight in bed, Jack leaned closer. "You're right, you won't get another chance. Far as I know, I thought I was the last Tracker. So that means now you're it. You're all we've got."

A prickle of unease crept alongside my excitement. "What do you mean?"

Jack hung onto my hand. "Which one of the vampires has made a bid for you, or have they both?"

My muscles clenched, and a mixture of fear and surprise shot through me. I leaned forward, lowering my voice. "How did you know?"

"Wolf, go shut the door." The Tracker commanded and Alex did as he was told, trotting over and slamming the door shut. "Lock it too."

Over the scrabbling of Alex's claws, Jack spoke. "You think I'm here by accident? The doctors are claiming its lung cancer, but I ain't never smoked a fucking day in my life. You know what stimulants do to us?"

That I did. "Something like smoking would send our hearts into overdrive, cranking our metabolism up to the point of having our hearts burst."

He nodded and went on. "There were two leaders of the vampire nation. Emperor and Empress. They have a child, one they've raised to be the heir. But before they could get their kid on the throne, they were killed by a usurper."

I knew what was coming, so I beat him to it. "Faris." Jack's eyes all but sparkled, a thread of life still beating strong in his ravaged body.

"Yes. Now there is a full-out battle coming between the two factions. You are the key. They will both vie for you."

I snorted. "Why? What can I do for them? They can't even turn me into a vampire."

A soft click and Alex got the door locked, then made his way into the bathroom. The faucet came on and then the slurping of water, followed by a splash. He'd be busy for a few minutes at least.

"You really don't know your limits, do you?" Jack asked softly, his eyes full of worry. "Shit. I can't teach it all to you, not in one session."

"Tell me what you can. Please. And I'll come back as soon as I can." I swallowed hard and spit out my biggest concern, one that weighed on me far more than Faris and any stupid vampire shindig I might get yanked into. "I've been trying to Track the missing kids, but I can't feel them. It's like they don't exist; like they've never existed."

Jack laughed, a choking gasp at the end that had me reaching for the call button. He waved me off. "Try now."

I didn't want to fail, but even more, I didn't want to fail in front of someone I'd prefer to impress. One deep breath and I reached for the kids, all twenty or so of them. Like a blinding beacon, I could feel them, dead, but still there. I was still able to Track their faded threads. Relief coursed through me, making me sag into my chair.

"You tried to Track them on your side of the water, didn't you?"

"No, when we were in the air. What does that have to—"

With another wave of a gnarled hand, he cut me off, his other hand tightening over my fingers.

"Large bodies of water, like an ocean, bar our ability to Track. There is no child you can't find, Rylee. You just have to be on the right side of the water."

I stood up with a jerk and reached for Berget before he'd even stopped speaking. Her life force blazed through me and with a sob I dropped to my knees. Golden sunlight and blue eyes beckoned to me, the scent of summer and the warmth of my little sister's love was a rush so heady I couldn't keep my eyes open.

She was alive! Oh my god, Berget . . . A hand patted my shoulder. "Hush now. You thought she was gone for good?" I must have spoken my thoughts, though I could barely pull them together. I clung to Berget's thread like a drowning man to a dingy. She was alive; I could take her home. I wasn't alone—my family wasn't all gone.

Shaking, I stood and turned to go, already formulating how to get to Berget. Forget the other children. They were dead; they could wait. Berget was alive and I was going after her. Right now.

Jack spoke, his words echoing mine in a twisted way. "Rylee, wait. There is so goddamned much more. Your sister can wait a few more minutes, can't she?"

I took in a long, slow breath, my heart beating as if I'd been sprinting. My back still to him, I said, "You don't understand."

"I do. Perhaps more than any other Tracker would. I was like you. My abilities came online long before I found someone to share their knowledge with me. Let me pass on what I know before you run off after her. Before I die."

Biting down, I clenched my jaw, turning to face him. "Quickly."

"It can't be fucking done quickly, but I'll give you what I can right now." He settled in back against his pillows. "You can Track more than a single person?"

I nodded, already figuring this lesson out for myself.

"You can also Track groups of people. Like a group of supernaturals. This is what the vampires want you for. You can find creatures that no one else can, that everyone thinks are gone."

I frowned, not understanding the significance of what he was saying. "So?"

He reached out for me, and I reluctantly let him take my hand. I wanted to go, Berget was so close!

His fingers dug in around my wrist. "You can help them Track their enemies, help them pinpoint people around them. You are a tool for them; remember that above all else. They will not see you for anything else. And if you don't work for them as they wish, they have no problem breaking their tools and finding new ones."

A chill swept through me. "That's what they did, broke you, and had me brought in?"

He nodded. "Give me one last thing, a last request."

Inwardly, I groaned, but I squeezed his hand in agreement.

"Go and find the missing children that I couldn't Track. That is my last wish. Do it before you find your sister. Prove you are a Tracker first, above all else."

9

Jack Feen's hand tightened over mine. "And once you have found your sister, come back to me. I don't want to fucking die alone in this bitch of a hospital."

Oh, for the love of all that was holy! I closed my eyes, fought the warring emotions. The logical part of my brain told me that he was right. I would never be able to get away from Valley and his minions to go after Berget. The missing infants and toddlers would have to come first. But the other side of me raged. To be this close, to be on the verge of finding the one person who meant more to me than any other, only to be denied, wasn't fair.

"I know it's fucking hard, Rylee. But you have to do what's right."

Giselle had said life wasn't fair, only that I should follow my heart, and Jack's words were echoing my beloved mentor's. And while my heart still loved Berget, I knew that I had to go after the other kids first. Jack was right. Son of a bitch.

"All right, I'll go after the kids."

He let out a long slow breath. "Good, that's all I ask of you."

A knock on the door and a muffled, "Ma'am?" on the other side interrupted us.

Alex let out a woof as if he were a guard dog. Yeah, not so much.

"A little late, buddy," I muttered, letting go of Jack's hand. The knock on the door came again, harder this time.

Striding to the door, I flicked the lock and opened the door. A police officer for sure by the way he held himself, but he was dressed in a suit, more like an FBI agent. A glimpse of a shoulder holster made me leery. On the off chance he wasn't an officer of some sort, he could be trouble. His eyes looked me over in a single, raking glance, his nostrils flaring ever so slightly like he didn't like what he saw. Well, piss on him too.

"Ms. Adamson, I'm here to pick you up and take you back to the police station."

His voice was smooth, the English accent soothing and soft. That made me wonder about Jack, who'd had no accent that I could discern. I'd have to ask him about that when I came back with Berget.

"How do I know you are who you say you are?" Sure I was being difficult, but also recognizing that he could be working for Faris. I'd have to watch everyone I came in contact with now. This was going to be difficult.

Lips tight, he pulled out his ID card and handed it over to me. William Gossard, SOCA, the symbol stamped on it was an attacking cat of some sort leaping over the earth. Funky.

"Doesn't mean jack shit to me. I could print this out at home."

His eyes lit up. "Just because you are ignorant, doesn't mean something isn't real. SOCA, Serious Organized Crime Agency. We're in charge of this particular case."

"Thought it was Interpol who called us in."

"We *are* a part of Interpol."

I could hear the fatigue in his voice. Like he'd been up all night and didn't appreciate explaining what he viewed as 'the basics' to me. Then again, maybe I was wrong.

Probably not.

"Right. I'm ready." I snapped my fingers and Alex bounded over to me, skidding to a stop, his eyes widening at the sight of the officer. Clapping his oversized paws on his muzzle he whispered out the corner of his mouth.

"Kitty shifter."

Kitty . . .? My body reacted while my brain was still spelling it out for me, and I yanked the knife from its sheath in my lower back. My big bowie knife was the next best thing to my swords, which I'd had to leave with Valley.

The officer narrowed his eyes, the color bleeding from a soft brown into a deep green. Interesting.

"Okay, so we have a problem. You showed me ID, but I still don't know you're here from the police." I had no doubt there were supernaturals around, lots in all sorts of fields. But it seemed too much of a coincidence that a shifter would come for me at the hospital. How did I know it wasn't one of Faris's cronies? Fuck, I did not want to start this day off with a fight and bloodshed.

The officer glared at me and the hair stood up on the back of my neck as a low growl, just like that of a pissed off kitty cat, rippled out of his lips.

"Ah, stop fucking around, the both of you," Jack yelled from the bed. "I'll vouch for Will. He's worked with me before. Now play nice, Rylee. He'll help you if you let him."

The shifter eased his stance, and then thrust out one hand. "Will Gossard."

I slid my blade back into its sheath, then slowly took his hand in mine. "Got that from the ID, genius." A pleasant heat tingled along his skin, danced across my fingers and settled into me. I snatched my hand back, but he seemed as surprised as I was. Interesting. Though I'd felt energy from other supernaturals upon meeting them, never anything quite so . . . intense.

Alex pushed me out of the way and held out one paw. "Alex."

Will blinked and looked over Alex's head to me. I shrugged. "Play nice with the doggy."

The two shifters 'shook' hands, and Alex seemed immensely happy, to the point of spinning in place.

"Alex, not now!" I bent and grabbed his dangling leash, and gave it a sharp jerk. He stopped and rolled on the floor, wiggling like a giant puppy.

A choked sound brought my eyes up. Will looked as though he was having a heart attack. His green eyes had faded back to hazel, but were wide with horror, and his face was pale.

I tightened my hand on the leash, bringing Alex to my side. "What?"

"You . . . you leashed him? Like a pet?" I could hear it in his voice, the fear of what I was capable of.

Perfect. At least he would show me some respect.

"Yup, and if you don't behave, I'll do the same to you." I bent down to Alex. "You'd like a kitty cat to play with, wouldn't you?"

The werewolf started to shake all over. "Yes! Kit-tyyyyyyyy!" He let out a long howl, and I clamped my hand over his muzzle. Too late. An alarm went off and I mentally cursed myself. Alex wouldn't have howled if I hadn't gotten him all riled up. Shit, that's what I got for poking at people.

Will shook his head. "The howl wouldn't have set the alarms off."

Jack let out a cough. "But a missing child would."

I swiveled back to him, my heart flooding with adrenaline. "What floor are the kids on?"

"Third."

I ran past Will, down the hallway, and hit the door to the stairwell at full speed, banging it open. Alex stayed right with me, and if the footsteps behind us were any indication, Will was close on our heels.

Two flights of stairs passed in a blur of seconds and we burst into the pediatric ward, the alarm going full tilt, a red light flashing over the desk. Will grabbed the closest nurse.

I loosened up the leash on Alex. "We've got to find that kid, buddy."

As serious as he ever got, he lowered his nose to the floor and immediately shook his head, scratching at the end of his muzzle. "Too many smells."

I didn't rebuke him for speaking. With everything that was going on, it would be a wonder if anyone noticed.

Will made a motion, and I followed him to the end of the hall. From outside one room I could hear sobbing, and a man's voice making an attempt to shush the crying. That would be the room we were looking for.

Stepping across the threshold, I squinted, checking my second sight for any nasty surprises. Nothing. That was good and bad. No surprise. Good. No clues. Bad.

"Excuse me, I'm sorry, but do you have a picture of your kid?" This was the part I hated, dealing with the parent. The father looked up, his face shell-shocked, short white blond hair sticking out in every direction.

"A picture?"

"Yes, we need to start circulating it immediately. And a name." I had no doubt that the cops that were even now rushing to the hospital would find nothing. Whoever was taking the kids knew what they were doing.

The father fumbled with his back pocket and I resisted the urge to hurry him up. Sure we were on a crunch, but there was no way the kid would be more than a block or two away.

He handed me a worn picture of a little boy, looked about two years old, same white blond hair as his father.

"Johnny, his name is Johnny. We only stepped out of the room for a split second and he was gone . . . I don't understand . . . ."

I reached for the kid, Tracking his threads, and sucked in a sharp breath. There was no way that was possible!

The kid was so far away I could barely feel him. Like he'd been somehow transported through space and time with the snap of a finger.

"Thanks," I said, tucking the picture into my pocket. With a sharp tug on Alex's leash, I snagged a small stuffed toy from Johnny's bed, then stepped back out of the room and leaned against the wall. So far away, so quickly, how was that possible? The only person I knew who had capabilities in that range was Charlie. Could it be a Brownie taking the kids? And if so, what the hell would they want with them?

Will moved up beside me and Alex crowded in close. "What are you picking up?"

"The kid is gone. Shit, whoever is taking them has some way to move them fast. Like as in some sort of . . ." I paused mid-sentence, not wanting to mention my other sudden suspicion, not yet at least. But there was another possibility. But no, no one would be that brassy. Would they?

Will's eyes tightened around the edges, his accent deepening. "You've thought of something."

"Any place to cross the Veil close by?"

He shook his head. "Not that I'm aware of. That doesn't mean there isn't." He frowned. "With buildings, it's usually in the basement or lower levels that the Veil is torn, closest to the earth."

"Then let's see what we've got below," I said, hanging onto Johnny's threads, feeling him slip further away with each second. Will gave a sharp nod and put his hand on my lower back, guiding me. Like I was some sort of princess. I pushed his hand off my back. "Just lead, man, no need to get touchy feely."

I wanted this case over so bad I could taste it. Berget was—I Tracked her—somewhere to the southeast. A distance for sure, but here in Europe, nonetheless.

We made our way down the stairwell, a flood of police officers going up as we went down. The fact that Will wasn't all that worried about the rules was good. Even I knew that we should have waited there to find out what the next step was with the local police detachment.

"Here," Will said, motioning at a door that, by the plaque, led into the boiler room. "This is the lowest room in the hospital."

I took the leash off Alex and let him sniff the teddy bear. "You smell Johnny down here?"

The werewolf lifted his nose to the air first, and then sniffed around our feet. With his head still down, tail straight out in line with his spine, he lifted one paw and pointed at the closed door. "Yuppy doody."

"He's quite the ham, isn't he?"

"You have no idea," I muttered. Opening the door, the three of us slipped inside. The furnace was going full tilt, the orange glow through the grills flickering light across the room.

"Spooky," I said.

Alex gave a shiver, rubbing his arms with his paws. "Spooky shit."

Will choked back a laugh. Score for Alex, he'd won over another person.

There was a heavy scent of mold and rot in the room, even though the boiler was running full tilt. Alex sniffed a couple of times, and then pinched his nose. "No like. Yucky."

I agreed. It was the kind of smell that clung to you, one of old graves and dead things; unpleasant was a freaking understatement. At least the room didn't take long to search. I Tracked the kid, and his life threads were already thinning. "He's going to die," I said, my heart breaking at the thought of the little one not only dying, but dying in the hands of a stranger.

A sharp spike of fear came through my connection to him, and then it faded, as he fell asleep, most likely a spell or a drug to knock him out.

"We can get to him in time," Will said, his determination admirable.

But I knew what was coming.

I shook my head. "I'm not giving up, but I can feel how close he is to death. He must have been hooked up to a respirator or something that was keeping him going. At the most, the kid's got five minutes. Maybe."

Will stared at me. "Just like that, you sentence him to death?"

Anger whipped up through me. "Fuck you. You don't know what I do, you can't possibly understand! I can feel his heart giving out, feel each beat getting weaker as if my fingers were right over his pulse. I've done this enough times to be able to read what's going to happen. He will die, and it won't be in vain because we're going to catch this son of a bitch who took him and make him pay. Got it?"

My yelling echoed through the small room. Will was visibly shaken and he took a half step back, lowering his eyes.

"Got it."

"Now let's find the threshold the bastard used to cross the Veil. That's a good start."

But no matter where we looked, there was nothing. No doorway, no break in the concrete. Running my fingers over the walls showed nothing. I even checked with my second sight—still nada. The walls were smooth and unblemished, regardless of how I looked at them. The furnace made the room almost unbearably hot, and sweat quickly slid down my face and arms. Fuck it all to hell and back!

"Now what?"

I didn't answer him, my hands on my hips; frustration mounting, I stared at the floor. The toddler was fading fast, and I reluctantly let go of his threads, and stopped Tracking him. Feeling a child die is a horrible thing, one that can't truly be described. I didn't need that, not today. I thought about the Lighteater I'd killed while Tracking him. That had been almost as bad as feeling a child die. Almost, but not quite.

"Back to the police station, I guess," I said quietly, knowing the next time I Tracked the toddler he'd be dead. Gods, this was an ugly world.

"Are you all right?"

Looking up, I caught his gaze as it softened with understanding.

"He's gone?"

I nodded and clamped down on the urge to cry. Stupid as it was, it didn't matter how many kids I'd

Tracked, this hurt never lessened regardless of the times I felt it. Lots of them passed on before I had even begun to Track them. And yet when a child died during a salvage, I felt it the most, like a keen blade taking another piece of me. It hurt, and I hadn't even met the kid.

Clearing my throat, I pointed at the door, "Let's go."

As we made our way back up the stairs, I thought about what O'Shea would do. Probably go and take a closer look at the files, see if there was some connection other than what the police had already found. Maybe find a motive. Damn him for opening my eyes. Life was a hell of a lot simpler when it was just about a salvage and not about the 'why' of a case.

Even though he wasn't with me, O'Shea was still making my life difficult.

And that made me smile, even if just a little.

10

The police station looked old, as in ancient times before modern anything. Lit inside by wall sconces that had obviously been converted from gas to electric, it was apparently not the main police station, but instead an office set up for Interpol and Will's division of SOCA. Will had filled me in on the way to the station. SOCA had a department set aside to deal with the supernatural, just like the FBI. And just like the FBI, that division of SOCA didn't truly exist in the hierarchy of things.

"Makes it hard to get things done, when you aren't taken seriously," Will said as we stood in the entryway of the station. "Not to mention the difficulty of working with humans who don't really believe in the supernatural."

"I can imagine that would be difficult," I muttered.

Will gave a wry smile. "You're about to find out just how difficult it can be. You're about to be introduced to the 'team' assigned to this case."

I didn't like the sound of that, but still I followed Will into the station, keeping Alex right with me. Even if this was the department for the supernatural goings on, I had no doubt that Alex would not be made welcome. Eyes followed us, none of them particularly friendly. Excellent.

"I see the welcoming party was laid out for me," I said.

Will snorted. "You aren't the only one they aren't happy with."

"Let me guess, you don't play well with others, either?"

He laughed, and I had to smile. Us supernaturals, we did our best to blend in, but the humans almost always picked up on something. Energy, weird traits, odd sayings, maybe just the way we talked or moved. Things that we thought nothing of, but to the rest of the world, well, we would never be like the rest of them. Which was just fine by me.

Weaving our way through the room, Alex got his share of wide-eyed glances too. But it wasn't until a heavyset older woman in a too tight bright red dress suit squealed and pointed that I thought we might have a problem.

"You can't bring a dog in here! People have allergies to dogs," she screeched, her accent so strong I struggled to understand her.

Alex lifted his one paw up and opened his mouth to speak. I could just hear him now. "Not dog, werewolf!"

I clamped a hand over his muzzle, stopping the flow of words that was coming. "He's a sniffer dog. And he's on the case, so shut your fat mouth." That last was directed at both the woman and Alex as my fingers tightened incrementally. He blinked up at me, winked in a big, slow comical blink of one eyelid, and I snickered, the laughter squeaking out past my clamped lips.

Will lifted an eyebrow and tipped his head toward the woman, whose face was almost as red as her suit. Ooops.

Sputtering, spit visibly flying from her lips, she said, "How dare you speak to me that way!"

Full-on laughing now, I managed to say, "Oh, piss off." Then I adjusted my grip on the leash and motioned for Will to continue leading the way. She wasn't my boss; if anyone wanted to make an attempt to bully me it would have to be Agent Valley.

Will did as I asked, I followed and we left the bright red woman shaking with rage behind. At least that was a positive.

He led us to a mid-sized office, big enough for ten or so people, of which it had almost double already. They all turned as we stepped inside the doorway, all those eyes taking us in. I met those eyes that I could, not willing to show weakness of any sort in front of this many suits.

Alex gave a low whimper and pressed into my side. Under his breath, so low I could barely hear him, he said, "Werewolf."

Ah, fuck, that would not be helpful. Of course, Valley would know that there was another werewolf involved in the investigation, wouldn't he?

I scanned the room, taking in the predominantly male, old, grumpy faces. Yup, my day just got that much harder. Will introduced me and my 'working' dog. I nodded my head, found Agent Valley and made my way over to him. This many people in such a tight space was too much, and I wasn't even claustrophobic.

A tall, thin, balding man rapped his knuckles on the small table in the middle of the room. "As most of you are aware, there was another kidnapping this morning. Officer Gossard was on scene. Can you fill us in on anything?" The tone implied that Will should have captured the criminal with one hand tied behind his back. These fucking humans, they just didn't understand what it meant to deal with a supernatural who stole children. There were no hard and fast rules when it came to magic and the world we lived in.

While Will spoke about what we'd done to try and track the kidnapper, I leaned down to Agent Valley.

"How much do they know about me?"

His lips barely moved. "Everything."

I closed my eyes and stood back up.

"Ms. Adamson?" My eyes opened, and I forced them to do so slowly. No need to let them get the upper hand.

"Hmm." I arched one eyebrow and lifted my hand in the air. "Present."

A low snicker went around the room.

"Would you care to share your particular findings?"

I shrugged and took a step forward like I would if I were called on in school, tucking my hands against my lower spine. "I Tracked the kid, Johnny, until he died. Everything else that happened, Officer Gossard already told you."

Silence met my words. Perhaps that wasn't the best way to pass on the info, but what the hell, I wasn't one of them, never would be.

The man licked his lips, frowning. "The child is dead?"

I didn't get a chance to answer. Alex did it for me, being helpful, as usual.

"Yesssirrrreee." He let the word end in a light howl, then his eyes flew to mine and he clamped his paws over his muzzle. "Sorry, Rylee. Alex forgets."

If I thought the room had been silent before, it was nothing to the emptiness that filled it after Alex spoke. I could almost feel the panic swirling into the air.

"Ah, fuck it. Someone else in here's a werewolf too, so don't get your panties in a twist that I brought one in," I said, motioning at the rest of the room with a broad sweep of my hand.

Now the panic let loose, grown men scrambling to get out of the room until it was the tall man, Agent Valley, Will, and one other Officer left with me and Alex.

Agent Valley shrugged. "I told you she was difficult, and you wanted all your Officers to get a good look at the supernatural Tracker. Well, now you did. Are you happy?"

Was he standing up for me? Booyah!

The tall thin man shook his head. "We can't have her going rogue on us, not after Feen. We have rules—we expect them to be followed."

Much as I wanted to tell him to take his rules and shove them up his ass, I thought I'd let Agent Valley speak up for me.

Which he did, in spades. I liked the short ugly man who wanted to be my boss better and better.

"She has a higher success rate than all of your officers and my agents combined. I'm inclined to let her do as she wishes" —he gave me a look that told me he wasn't really giving me free rein at all— "within reason."

Will stepped forward. "I'll keep an eye on her. I can partner with her while she works the case."

Alex clapped his paws and his tail thumped. Out the side of his mouth he did a stage whisper. "I like the kitty."

The other man—the one sitting in the corner— stood up, anger darkening his features. His head was shaved to the wick and his eyes were hooded, hiding the color from me, but I'd have laid money at that moment they were a tawny yellow. "You bitch, who do you think you are collaring a werewolf?"

He stalked toward me and my normally submissive Alex stiffened against my leg, his body inching forward. "No mean to Rylee!"

"Smith, ease down," the tall man said, motioning for the werewolf, Smith, to sit.

Surprisingly enough, he did. Good to know. Perhaps he wasn't a true Alpha?

"Alex, enough," I said, lowering hand to the top of his head.

"Boss said take care of you. Keep Rylee safe," he said, scratching at his ear with a back foot, the 'almost' confrontation already forgotten.

My heart squeezed. O'Shea, he meant O'Shea had told him to look out for me.

The other men were talking and I overheard Agent Valley call the tall man Denning.

I grabbed a chair and slumped into it, Alex sitting beside me with his head on my knee. Smith glared at me from across the room and I stuck my tongue out at him.

Alex mimicked me, then proceeded to make progressively worse faces until Smith looked away with a glower. Chuckling to myself, I put a hand on Alex's head, rubbing him behind his ears.

Will pulled a chair up beside me. "What do you think we should do next?"

"It would be nice if we could figure out what kind of supernatural is taking the kids."

"Are you so sure it isn't a human?"

I snorted. "What human is going to know about crossing the Veil, and not just crossing it, but using it as a means to travel? And has the ability to hide the entrance to the Veil so well that in a ten by twelve room the two of us couldn't find it?"

He was silent.

"Besides," I said, "they wouldn't have brought me in for a serial kidnapper unless there was a supernatural element."

"Are you so sure about that?"

I thought for a moment about the group of men that had been in the room to gawk at me. No doubt Jack Feen would never have stood for that kind of reception. As if reading my mind, Will spoke.

"Jack was a little more low key than you. He only had a few contacts within the agency. Worked with me for the most part and didn't like Denning all that much. And he never came into the office. Ever."

Glancing over at the verbally sparring men, I could see why. Denning was arguing that I had to be on a short leash, controlled like the wild card I was. Agent Valley was arguing for me to do what I had to and worry about the consequences later. Maybe O'Shea had been wrong about his boss, or maybe he'd changed since losing his number one agent to the world of the supernatural.

I leaned my head back against the wall behind me and closed my eyes. Jet lag was finally kicking in and it looked like it was going to be a bitch.

Welcome to London, Rylee.

Milly crooked her finger, and O'Shea stepped forward, his innards twisting with fury. But all that moved was a subtle twitch over his right eye. She'd commanded him to get into her car, and drove deep into the badlands to the old mining shaft where Rylee and he had crossed the Veil, looking for India in what seemed like forever ago.

He'd done what Milly asked him to without hesitation, unable to stop his body from reacting to her commands. When they reached the mineshaft, there were still remnants of police tape, and he could smell the blood and viscera under the snow as if it were fresh and not months old.

"Come now, don't fight this," Milly said. "In the end, this is better. You have to trust me."

Of course, he couldn't so much as utter a god-blasted grunt without her giving him a command to speak. Witch or not, Rylee's best friend or not, he'd rip her throat out the second the torc was off. She commanded him to slip on a repelling harness and pick her up, which he did; and then they went over the edge of the shaft and slid into the darkness.

"Careful now," Milly said, her voice close to his ear. "You aren't just carrying my life in your hands, but one other too."

He could flick his eyes over to hers, and though there was little light he had no problem seeing the glint there. The glow of happiness.

No. Fucking. Way.

Finally, after what seemed like hours of arguing, Denning let me and Agent Valley go. With nearly free rein. Will was to stick with me at all times, and Officer Smith was to be our third. That stuck in my craw like a sideways fishbone.

"Another werewolf is not a good idea," I hissed at Agent Valley as we strode through the precinct to the area that had been set aside for us.

"I couldn't get him to back down," Agent Valley snapped back at me, and then smoothed out his hair. "As it was, I could barely get him to agree to you having the lead on this."

Though it galled me, I knew he'd done the best he could. "Yeah, thanks for that."

Flipping a stack of files on a desk, he pointed to the chair. "Sit, read. Figure this the fuck out, Adamson. And when you're ready to Track the kids, let us know. But the last thing you are to do is go out on your own. Got it?"

Lips pursed tight, I gave him a half nod. I wanted to Track the kids *now*, by myself, and get the job done. Then I could go after Berget. Letting out a deep breath, I flopped into the squeaky chair and flipped open the first file. None of the information was new, just a re-hashing of the same stuff I'd already read: the kids, their ages, parents and siblings. Nothing new. Was this what being a part of the FBI was about? Pushing paper around until your eyes crossed and you hoped all to hell and back that you caught something? Ugh. I'd made the right choice; I could never do this on a regular basis. A snore from Alex at my feet made me glance down. He wasn't the only one feeling the twist from the jet lag. Stifling a yawn, I put my head down on my desk and covered my hair with my hands. Gods, why not just go after the kids now, get it done?

Because you need to know what you're dealing with. And you need to know why the kids are being snatched so you can stop it and keep it from happening again. O'Shea's voice seemed to echo in my head. Damn him, even when he wasn't here he was right.

A hand touched my shoulder and I flinched. I was too tired to even keep my guard up. Not a good sign.

Will bent over me with a cup of coffee. "Jack never liked coffee, but I thought maybe you'd want some?"

"No." I ran my hands through my hair. "I need to sleep."

"Right. I can take you to where you're staying. Just down the street in a basement suite."

Again, he led the way, me only half awake behind him. Alex stumbled along too. Though only late afternoon here, we'd left yesterday, and at home it was the middle of the night; I'd been up way too long.

Rain pattered down around us, dark grey clouds pressing in from above, giving me the impression of endless grey. Two blocks down from the precinct, Will paused. "Here's your key, go right in. I believe all your weapons were brought here by Agent Valley." He handed me the key and a card. "That's my number on there, call me when you get up and we can get started first thing in the morning."

I nodded, took the key, mumbled "thanks" and opened the door. The inside was dim, but the walls were painted a cheery blue that matched the curtains, carpet and furniture. Matchy, matchy—how vomit inducing. Locking the door behind me, I propped a chair under the handle. Call me paranoid, but if Faris wanted me on his team, I had no doubt I'd be paid a visit sometime soon.

My weapons bag was still locked and I slid a small key out of my pocket. Opening up the hard-backed case, I took a quick stock of my weapons. I'd mostly brought blades in various sizes, my two swords being foremost amongst those. Silver threaded whip, cuffs, throwing knives, flak jacket, and my newest hobby, full size crossbow and bolts. I wasn't one-hundred percent that it would work, it might be too mechanical, but my test shoots had been clean, so I was going to give it a try. There were more than a few badasses out there I'd like to kill at a distance. And it would keep my dry cleaning bill down.

With a deep sigh I pulled one sword free and started through the forms of fighting Giselle had taught me, mostly Muay Thai. Block, parry, thrust, elbows, knees, fist, and feet. Over and over until my body hummed with the movements. Then I picked up the second sword and worked my way through a few more imaginary opponents. Sweating, I slid out of my leather jacket and dropped to the floor, forcing myself through sit-ups, push-ups, and a variety of other strength training exercises. Sure I was exhausted, but I had to be fit, ready to go after the kids that I was Tracking. Because no matter that I had some supernatural abilities, I was no fucking Superwoman. I could be hurt and killed as easily as anyone else. That was one lesson I was reminded of on almost every salvage, picking up new scars to add to the history already written on my body with blades, teeth, and claws.

Finally done with my routine, I hopped in the shower for a quick wash. Stepping back into the main room, I dressed in clean clothes, and then picked up one sword and slid it under my pillows. I left the sheath on the sword. The edge of it was spelled to cut deep, but I'd slept with my weapons more than once and had learned the hard way to keep the sheath on unless I was fighting or practicing. I climbed into bed, pulled the blue comforter up to my chin, and let out a deep sigh. Exhausted, the last thing I did was Track Berget. Her energy and excitement flowed through me. She was happy, that at least was good. Whoever had taken her had taken good care of her. There was no fear in her at all.

A smile swept across my lips; it wouldn't be long and I'd finally have my sister back. Closing my eyes, I sunk into the world of sleep.

11

The next morning did not dawn bright and cheery. A freaking cloud-ridden, storm-filled sky greeted me and Alex as we stepped out of our blue suite. The light drizzle dampened my hair to my head, and within minutes my face dripped water like I was standing under a faucet. Alex seemed happy though, sniffing the air and yanking on the leash to pull me along, oblivious to the bad weather with his thick coat and naturally happy attitude.

"Ease up, buddy," I grumbled. I'd slept like the dead, but I still had a hard time waking up, feeling as though my limbs were tied down with weights. Shit, this jet lag business was a bitch.

"Alex hungry."

"When we get to the station. And stop talking," I said just as we passed an older couple walking with their umbrella's held high. The woman pointedly kept her gaze averted, but the man had no problem giving me a grumpy look. I glared back at him. Good, I didn't particularly feel like being nice anyway.

The station was quiet, with only a few officers at their desks when we got there. I weaved my way through the main room to the desk I'd been assigned the day before and sat down. Alex whimpered at my feet.

Pointing to his belly he whispered, "Alex really, really hungry. Going to die!"

On cue, his stomach let out a rolling grumble.

"You have to wait for Will."

Throwing himself to his belly, his limbs splayed out as if he were a trophy rug, he said, "Stupid late kitty."

Laughing to myself, I pulled the files out and started to go through them, my eyes taking everything in, my head listening to O'Shea's voice.

Check again. Something small, something only you would notice. That's what you're looking for.

I was halfway through my next go round with the files when Will showed up, fast food in hand.

Alex shot up to stand on his back feet, making gimme gestures with his claws. Will tossed him a bag and the werewolf dropped down, chowing the greasy food with gusto.

"And you didn't call me because . . .?" Will handed me a can of orange juice and a bagel with cream cheese.

Spreading the cream cheese in a thick layer, I took a bite of the bagel, speaking around the mouthful. "Figured you would be at work. Thanks for breakfast."

Will smiled. "You're welcome. Now, what can I do to help?"

I handed him the half of the files I'd gone through twice already. "Read, find similarities, or do whatever it is that cops do to break cases."

He took the files and we got down to work. Boring, pointless, ridiculous work that made me want to scream in frustration. I Tracked Berget while I worked, felt her emotions skim along mine. She was happy, healthy, her threads were strong and vibrant. How would our reunion be? Would she be happy then? Or was she happy in her life as it was? The fear that perhaps she might not want to come back with me hit me between the eyes like an unexpected hammer blow. A possibility I hadn't considered until that moment. I mean, it's not like I'd be taking her back to a happy family unit. Our world had been destroyed when she'd gone missing . . . there was a very good chance she had a better life where she was than if she came back with me. Fuck it all to hell.

Jerking to my feet, I gripped the edge of the desk, the room seeming to sway as I struggled to get in a good breath. "I've got to go for a walk, get some fresh air," I said, not liking the way my voice sounded.

Breathy and out of control, clamping down on my emotions, I motioned for Alex to stay behind. Will could look after him for a few minutes; I needed to be alone.

Head down, I burst out onto the sidewalk, gulping the cool air, the now sleeting half-rain, half-snow coursing down my cheeks. The moisture quickly turned from just wet to miniature ice crystals that stabbed at me. My steps were silent on the wet pavement as I walked, my brain rushing around the idea that Berget might be happier without me, without her family. Why did that have to hit me now? Shit, this was not the time to be freaking out.

"Come on, Rylee, pull it together," I said softly. I stepped onto a grassy embankment, working my way to a long stone and wrought iron fence. Finding handholds, I climbed over, and dropped on the other side without a sound. Blinking, I wiped rain from my eyes and took a sharp breath.

The cemetery was old, as in older than anything I'd ever been in before. In the far distance I could see a church, the bell tolling the hour, and closer was a caretaker's hut. Picking my way around the graves, the scent of mold and death greeted me, curled around my senses, and brought the smell seeping from my memories.

It smelled just like the boiler room, exactly like what the supernatural left behind after snatching Johnny. There was a short list of supernaturals who frequented graveyards and only one I knew of strong enough to make children disappear as they were. And no, it wasn't a vampire. Contrary to popular fiction, vampires aren't much into graveyards and coffins.

The problem was, even I didn't know much about this particular supernatural I was suspecting, so if I was right, I was going to be in for some surprises.

Breaking into a jog, I was at the caretaker's hut in no time, banging on the door. Suspicions were all I had, but *if* I was right, I at least knew what we were dealing with when it came to the kidnapper. Or at least it was a start.

"Hello? Anyone home?" I banged my fist on the door again, rattling the thin wood on its hinges.

A muffled voice shouted out at me. "Bloody hell, give me a minute to get me pants on!"

I stepped back as the door opened, an older man with long grey hair and squinting eyes peeking out at me.

"What you want? A burial?" He shooed at me with his hands, "Go to the church, they do the arranging of burials for you. I just dig the hole."

He started to close the door and I put my hand on it, stopping him. "No, I'd like to ask you a question. Do you get many grave robbers here?"

His eyebrows shot into his hairline and I thought perhaps I'd been wrong. Staring at me, he shook his head. Damn it, I'd thought I'd been on to something. Looked like I was back to square one.

I turned to walk away when his voice stopped me.

"How did you know?"

I spun around. "Know what?"

"About the graves that have been disturbed. Robbed isn't quite the right word for what happened here."

"Will you tell me about them, the disturbances?" Fingers crossed, this could be the break I needed.

He beckoned me in. "No one would take me seriously, just brushed me off like I was a crazy old coot."

I followed him into his hut, the heat from an antique pot belly stove taking the chill out of the air.

"I'm the caretaker here. Name's Harold. Have a seat." He pointed to a solidly built chair.

I lowered myself into it. "I'm Rylee."

"Good name. Warrior name, I think," he mumbled as he bent and rifled through a box next to the stove. "Was going to burn these papers, just never got around to it."

With an almost casual toss, he flopped a stack of papers onto the table in front of me.

Each paper contained a number, name, and date, along with pictures in many cases. There were over a hundred sheets.

Harold pointed at the paper on top. "That number there designates the grave, the name of the deceased, and the date the grave was disturbed."

"Why do you have all these? I mean, I understand you're the caretaker, but this is . . ." I looked at the stack of pages, knowing without counting that there were a lot. More than just keeping records. "Extremely detailed."

Giving me a smile, he looked over my shoulder, as if seeing things that weren't really there. "My pa was a details kind of man. Taught me the importance of keeping things until they were no longer needed. If you'd been a day or so later, might be that all these would be gone."

I flipped through the pages quickly, staring at the few pictures that Harold had pinned to the pages. Each grave looked not as if it had been dug up, but more like it had been *dug out*. Like whatever had been in the grave had clawed its way to the surface.

Gripping the paper, a shot of excitement zipped through me. "Can you show me some of these graves?"

Harold bobbed his head, and then grabbed his coat. "But you know, they stopped—all the grave robberies stopped. Haven't had one in, oh, about—"

I finished it for him. "The last two years?"

Blinking his squinty eyes of indiscriminate color up at me, he smiled. "Yup, that's right on the mark. You a bobby?"

Staring at him blankly seemed to get my point across that I had no idea what he was talking about. He cleared his throat and clarified. "A police officer?"

"Private investigator," I answered without hesitation.

"Ah, I see. Makes sense, the police, they're too busy to be bothered with grave robberies. Too busy by far."

He grabbed two umbrellas and handed me one. But the weather wasn't bothering me anymore. Shit, this was why O'Shea liked to ask questions. Because when the puzzle pieces came together it was a freaking high like no other!

We made our way around the graveyard, Harold pointing out the graves that had been disturbed. All of them were children, all under five years old, with the exception of one—the oldest grave.

From close to a hundred years ago, the kid was the oldest of the group as well. Twelve years old, a girl, and—I bent to read the tombstone better—she died of the wasting disease.

Brittany Mariana Tolvay. Nothing else but her name and the dates. No, that wasn't true. I bent down and brushed the grass back from the base, the words faded with age and weather, but I could read them still.

Beloved daughter. Cleansed by fire in the hands of God. Gone for but a moment.

"This one was dug out?" I pointed at it, not sure if what I was seeing fit or not.

Harold stepped forward. "That one there is strange, the only one where it looked like a proper grave robbing. Someone trying to get in."

But if the kid's body had been burned, there wouldn't have been anything left to steal. This was the only one that didn't fit with the others. This was the starting point.

I shook myself. No, what I was seeing confirmed my suspicions. I had some proof, and I was ready to rumble. The asshole stealing kids from their death-beds was about to get a nasty surprise on his doorstep.

I saw Harold back to his hut, thanked him for his help, and turned to go, papers tucked inside my jacket; but something pulled at me, like string tied around my waist, I felt it vibrate under my skin.

Standing quietly, I let my senses guide me. Some-one was throwing around a lot of power, so much so that even my miniscule abilities with detection were picking it up. The church bells tolled and I frowned. The time was wrong for the bells to be tolling. Hell, it was twenty-two minutes passed the hour, not even close. And churches were, if nothing else, particular about their rituals.

Setting out once more in a brisk walk, I made my way to the church, feeling the power of whoever it was grow the closer I got. Like a wash of home, I felt the hum of magic and knew it was a witch battling it out in the church. For one brief second, I wondered if it was Milly. But no, whoever this was throwing power around was stronger even than Milly; besides Milly was an ocean away, it wouldn't be her.

The bells tolled again, and this close, the sound rumbled through my chest. Leaning up against the huge wooden doors, I pressed my ear tight against them. Chanting, a lot of chanting. My skin crawled in remembrance. The last time I'd been on the other side of a set of doors and chanting we'd almost lost a little girl, India in fact, to a serious demon possession.

Though I doubted that was the case now, I still couldn't turn around and just leave without making sure whoever was being chanted over was okay.

With a shove, I opened the double doors wide and strode in, stopping in the vestibule, the scene before me not something I'd expected.

Two circles of priests surrounded a girl strapped down on the altar; a cloth was draped over her body and a chunk of wood, what I was betting was a heavy wooden cross, was on her chest. One priest held a bowl over her head as he chanted, then slowly poured the water out on her face.

She snapped her head to the side. "Get the hell off me!" Her English accent made me think of the girl from Harry Potter. Hermione, if I remembered the name correctly.

The priests, of course, didn't listen, nor did they listen as she flicked her wrist and sent one of them flying into the air. They had no idea what they were dealing with.

"You should let her go," I said loudly, and the church went silent.

Stepping down out of the vestibule and into the main alley between the pews, I ran my fingers over the wooden armrests. "She isn't possessed and you have no right to torment her."

Two priests came toward me, faces grim, the one on the right doing all the talking. "Her family gave her to the church to heal. Now be gone with you." They shooed at me like I was a stray dog.

I smiled and slid my two swords from the crossed sheath at my back. "I don't play nice, boys."

They stopped their advance on me and it was my turn to motion for them to get out of my way. They listened, stepping back.

The head honcho, the one with the fancy scarf around his neck and ridiculous looking hat, lifted his hand to me, palm out. "God will not be denied, and no matter the temptations that the devil will send, we will be faithful and bring this child to the light of Christ."

I lifted my middle finger to him. "This ain't got nothing to do with God or Christ. Now. Let. Her. Go."

The priest's eyes blazed with anger; I just continued to smile. This was about to get fun. I wouldn't really kill any of the priests, but that didn't mean they wouldn't make for some good practice. I put my swords back into their sheaths one at a time. There were nine priests, just enough to make this interesting.

I beckoned to the high priest, or whatever the fuck he was. "You're going to have to take me out before I let you put one more drop of holy water on her."

The church went even more silent, as if everyone held their breath, as if the air and tension from the tombs below had crept upward.

Mr. High Priest with the funky scarf and stupid hat made a motion with his left hand toward me. "Take her. We must not be interfered with; the child's soul is at stake."

Let the fun begin.

Hands circled around my waist in an attempt to keep my arms pinned. I snapped my head backwards, connecting with his nose, the crunch of cartilage crackling through the air, blood hitting the back of my neck. He screamed and let go. Spinning, I jerked my right foot up, catching the second priest under his chin, and knocking him out cold. Damn, that was over way too fast.

Dusting off my jacket, I turned and lifted an eyebrow at the remaining priests. "Anyone else care for a go?"

Six of the remaining seven moved toward me, spreading out through the pews. Perfect. Hopping up onto the pew closest to me, I ran toward the closest priest, dropping my weight, and sliding along the wooden bench, as he swung a sloppy right hook at me.

"Let me guess, you've got mommy issues. That's why you're a priest," I said, spinning on my butt and pinning the priest to the pew in front of us. He glowered at me and I booted him hard in the chest, knocking the breath out of him. As he slid down, a second kick to the jaw made his eyes roll back in his head.

Moving quickly, I dispatched the next two priests with ease, leaving three young men who looked like they were fresh out of seminary, two of the three covered heavily in pimples.

"Listen, I can kick your asses and you can wake up tomorrow morning uglier than you are now . . ." I paused to let them take that in, "or you can fuck off and keep what's left of your pride."

They grouped tighter together and slowly advanced.

Smiling, I said, "Alrighty then."

I unhooked my whip and let the tail drop to the floor, the leather shushing along the wood as I walked.

A flick of my wrist snapped the whip into the air, and I pulled down hard with my whole arm to crack the leather tip over their heads. They scattered like a herd of sketched out cows, running for the exits.

Laughing softly, I tucked the whip away and turned to face the final priest who, no doubt, wished he had some magical powers of his own right then.

"You are of the devil and I cast you out," he yelled, flicking holy water at me.

I couldn't stop the laugh that leapt out of me. "Oh my. Please, throw some more lukewarm water on me. I'm trembling with fear all the way down to my tight little ass."

The high priest shook with what I could only assume was rage as he started in on the Latin.

I cleared my throat, then held up a hand to him and miracle of miracles, he stopped. "Listen, I'm going to take the girl, and you're going to say that she ran away. Got it?"

"She is my charge! I cannot—"

My sword cleared its sheath, the blade slicing through the air so fast he couldn't dodge it; I held the tip against the hollow of his throat. "You can. She doesn't belong with you in your world. She belongs in mine."

He opened his mouth to speak, and I stepped closer; let him see my tri-colored eyes as they swirled.

Stuttering to a stop he stepped away. "Get thee gone. And take the devil child with you."

I saluted him with my sword. "Excellent."

Two swift slices and the girl was free of her bonds. She slithered off the altar, clutching the tablecloth over her. The priest snatched it away. "Do not touch the emblems of Christ!"

"Stuff a sock in it," I said, as I held my hand out to the girl.

Barely covered with a thin sack-like dress that hung to the floor, she stood in the shadows of one of the stained glass windows, the faint midday light coming through doing nothing to give me a better look at her. Blazing blue eyes glared at me, and though I felt her power swirl around me, it did nothing. Her eyes widened and I smiled at her. "You can't hurt me. Not like you do the others."

"I don't want to come with you."

Ignoring the priest and his muttering, I kept my focus on the girl. She made me think of Berget. They were so similar in coloring with the blonde hair and almost shocking blue eyes, but this girl, from what I could see of her, was rail thin, all angles and points. It looked as though they'd been starving her, the bastards. If she'd been a little older or better trained, they never would have been able to tie her down. They were lucky she hadn't killed them by accident.

"Well, here's the thing," I said, putting a hand on the altar and swinging across it to sit with my legs dangling on the other side. "You don't really fit in this part of the world, do you?"

Her eyes narrowed.

I went on. "And I'm betting your family just dumped you here, once your temper tantrums got out of control?"

"They weren't temper tantrums!" Tears starting to leak out of her eyes, the first I'd seen since I'd stepped into the church. This was one tough little kid. She reminded me a little of myself.

I softened my voice. "No, they weren't. But that *is* what they thought, isn't it?"

Gulping back a sob, she gave one short nod.

"Come on, kid. Let's get you out of here."

In my heart, I was crying with her. To be abandoned by your family, to have them walk away from you because you were a freak, that was a wound that would never truly heal—and if it did, it would scar her deeply. I would find her a place to learn, to study and hone her skills. Somewhere safe. Maybe the Coven back home. Now that I knew they weren't what Milly claimed, they would probably welcome the kid with open arms.

Sniffling, she reached out for my hand.

I covered her fingers with my own. "I won't let anyone hurt you. I promise." Dangerous words, but she needed that. I could see it in her.

She lifted her eyes to mine. "My name is Pamela."

"I'm Rylee. Or as dipshit over here would say, 'The Devil.'"

"You admit it!" He screeched.

I was rewarded with Pamela stepping out of the shadows and nailing him with a pure bolt of power, flipping him ass over tea kettle and into the far wall with a thud.

"Easy kid," I said, pushing her hands down.

"He hurt me," she whispered, staring at where he lay.

My hackles went up, anger spilling through my body, but what she said next slowed me down.

"And that should even the score."

I smiled at her. "Come on, let's go."

She took two steps fully into the light, her socks peeking out from under the long sack dress. Shocked beyond the ability to speak, all I could do was stare at her bright blue socks.

12

Milly had him carry her through the Veil and into the castle where they'd first found India. He was unable to do anything physical to stop what was happening, but his mind formulated plan after plan. He just needed to . . . what? He had no way to break this spell Milly had on him. Not unless he could get the torc off his neck.

"I don't want you to hate me, Liam. I know Rylee loves you. And she's like family to me."

He could hardly believe the lies pouring from her lips; was she really going to try and explain this backstabbing behavior?

Milly directed him up the stairs, through the castle, and out the front gates where there was, of all things, a horse drawn carriage waiting for them.

They stepped in and the carriage rolled forward before Milly spoke again. "I don't want to hurt her, but she needs to see, to understand how deadly a game she is playing without even knowing it."

O'Shea closed his eyes. At least he had that much control. At the moment, anyway.

The witch kept talking. "Faris, he's special. He will be the new emperor. And I will be his counselor." She paused. "You may speak your mind."

"Are you fucking nuts?" O'Shea roared.

Milly lifted an eyebrow. "Crazy? No. Pragmatic? Yes." She smoothed her clothes out over her body, hands lingering near her belly button, confirming his suspicions and freaking him out at the same time.

"You're pregnant with the vampire's child?"

She burst out laughing, leaning her head back and giving him a perfect view of her throat. The image of his teeth burying into the slim white column burned into his mind, giving him something to look forward to. Particularly if it was the vampire's child she carried.

"No," Milly said, her eyes softening. "Ethan's child. He's the leader of the Coven I was a part of."

O'Shea said nothing, and she went on as if he'd encouraged her.

"Ethan is the most powerful warlock in the western hemisphere."

"So you threw your family under the bus for a lay? I hope it was worth it." O'Shea said, glaring at the sultry, slutty witch.

She glared back. "I love him, and he loves me, regardless of his past. And as soon as he can, he's going to come here to be with me and the baby."

He smiled, a mere baring of his teeth; then laughed. "Let me guess, he had a wife and he told you that he would leave her for you? That you were the one he'd been waiting for? Please, with all the men you've fucked, you can't tell me you actually bought that line?"

"You don't know him! He'd not like the others. He won't leave me. Besides his wife is already dead," she said, her green eyes snapping with anger.

"Why'd you let me speak? You didn't think I'd actually agree with you, did you?"

"No, I didn't. But every man on death row should be allowed to have a final say."

Her words hit him square in the chest, sucking the air from him. Fighting against whatever spell held him against his will did nothing, his muscles didn't even tremble in response to his demand to move.

Milly leaned forward and ran a finger along his jaw. "What, you didn't think I was going to let you live, did you? Rylee won't let Faris help her until she's alone, until she has nowhere else to turn for help. You're going to kill Alex, and then Rylee will kill you. That will break her and make her open to Faris's advances. Which is what I, and my true master, wish."

She thought she had it all planned out? Fuck, he had to keep her talking, there had to be a weakness.

"You don't know her very well if you think that. She'll kill you for this, Milly."

"Not when I'm pregnant, she won't." Her self-satisfied smile grated across his nerves.

"What about Eve and Giselle?"

"I left something, a surprise for Eve. Giselle . . ." she closed her eyes and pressed her fingers to them, the first sign of remorse he'd seen. "Giselle will be last. It will be a mercy to end her life."

Lowering his voice, he all but growled at her. "You are going to die, witch. A long, slow, painful death, and one that your vampire, or true master, whoever the hell he is, won't save you from. Because in the end, they don't give a shit about you. You've bet on the wrong horse. You should have bet on Rylee."

The carriage lurched over a bump and she raised her hand to him, her power curling around his upper body. "You forget your place, wolf. You are no long an FBI agent—you're hardly even a man. You should try to remember that while we're here."

Through grit teeth, he asked the final question before she silenced him once more, "Where is here, exactly?"

She smiled. "London."

Pamela sat with her legs dangling off the edge of the chair, a sandwich in one hand, can of pop in the other, Alex staring up at her from the floor with big begging eyes and whispered pleas for her to share. We'd found her some clothes to replace the sack that had been masquerading as a dress, and a pair of shoes that sort of fit, but all I saw were her blue socks, like a beacon to my eyes. Giselle had been raving about blue socks for the last few months, but surely this was a coincidence? No, even I knew better than to question this chain of events. Pamela was needed, and the only thing Giselle had been able to see of her in the future was her blue socks. I shook my head. Unbelievable. A last gift from my mentor, one that I'd have never seen coming, not in a million years.

Will touched my right elbow, drawing my attention to him. "You can't keep this girl. We've got to return her to her family."

I felt more than saw Pamela still. "We don't even know her last name, so how are we supposed to track down her family?" I hoped she picked up the hint.

Will bent down, crouching in front of the young witch. "Honey, what's your last name?"

Her eyes met mine over his head. "I don't remember." Good girl.

Will turned his head to glare at me.

I shrugged. "I didn't say a thing."

"You didn't have to."

"I think I know what we're after; what's taking the kids." A change of subject was needed and this was a legit switch of topics. I shifted closer, lowering my voice. If I was wrong, I'd look like a fool in front of all these suits. Not something I was eager to experience, so for now it would be just between me and Will.

He closed the gap between us, his hands just suddenly resting on my hips, his lips moving very little. "If we look like we're having an affair, people won't take you seriously."

"They also won't follow me around if they think I'm sneaking off to get laid. It'll mean I can move around more freely," I said, also moving my lips as little as possible.

His hands slipped around my waist, totally inappropriate in any circumstance, and I could *feel* the stares from around the room settling on us. The thing was, I felt nothing, no tingle, no flush of heat. Will was handsome, young, available.

But he wasn't Liam. Not by a long shot.

"Necromancer." I said.

Will actually jerked away from me, his eyes bugging. "You're shitting me."

"Nope."

"Do you have proof?"

I pulled the papers that Harold the caretaker had given me and slid them across the desk. I kept my voice low. "Here you go. Pictures and everything. The grave 'robberies' stopped right around the time the kids started to go missing from the hospitals. Seems like our boy was looking for fresher meat."

Before Will could pick up the papers, Alex whimpered and scooted closer to Pamela. Watching them interact, it was interesting to see how quickly she accepted the supernatural. Then again, I'd been the same way when Giselle had found me. I'd accepted it within days, less maybe. It seemed that kids just saw what they saw and it became a part of their world almost seamlessly. Unlike the adults who got introduced to the supernatural. My thoughts again drifted to O'Shea. He'd caught on; it had just taken a while.

Pamela held up a piece of bologna from her sandwich. "Alex, sit." He sat up, tail thumping.

"Now, lay down." He flopped flat to the ground, all four limbs sprawled straight out.

"Roll over." The werewolf rolled across the floor and right into the red clad legs of the woman who'd screamed at us when we first arrived. She tumbled to the floor with a screech that made Alex clap his paws over his ears and howl.

Pamela giggled, one hand covering her lips, shoulders hunched as she laughed.

I jumped into the fray and yanked Alex away from the woman, who was still screeching.

"Are you all right?" I bent over the woman, not normally so worried about the stunts Alex pulled, but after the incident with O'Shea, I was hyper aware of the possibilities that could arise from a simple cut or even a scratch.

The woman jerked her arm away from me and clambered to her feet, her hair—which had previously been in a tight bun—in complete disarray. "Do not touch me."

I lifted my hands up, palms facing her. "Fine. I was trying to be nice."

She brushed past me and clamped a hand down on Pamela's shoulder. "I'm here to escort this child to her foster home. Until we can find her family, she will be in protective care."

Pamela pulled back, or at least tried to. "I don't want to go. I want to stay here." Her eyes pleaded with me.

Shit, this was about to get ugly. I could feel it just under the surface of my skin.

I cleared my throat. "Ms. . . .?"

The woman in red glared at me. "It's Dr. Daniels."

Great, a PhD and an attitude. Bad combination when it comes to dealing with people. Of course, I wasn't exactly known for my tact at the best of times. But for the kid, I would try.

"Dr. Daniels, Pamela doesn't want to go. Doesn't she get a say in her own life?"

The doctor snorted. "She's a child. She knows nothing of what is good for her and what isn't."

Pamela glared up at her. "I'm almost fourteen. I'm not a child. And I don't want to go with you." I could feel her power surging, and I shook my head at her.

"Pamela, don't do that," I said.

Dr. Daniels looked at me, then Pamela and back again. "Don't do what?"

We were saved by Will. "Excuse me, but Pamela is integral to our current case. We believe she may have information regarding the missing children, that there may be a connection between her case and theirs. Therefore, she is required by law and under the legislation of SOCA to be remanded into police custody until we are satisfied that we have all the information we need." He reached out and put a hand on Pamela's other shoulder.

The good doctor did not look amused. "I'm well aware of the law and legislation, Officer Gossard. But the child's welfare is my concern. She will be going with me. Immediately."

Now it was my turn. We'd played nice and, as happened most often, nice wasn't going to cut it.

I pushed my body between Pamela and the doctor's, forcing her hand off the kid's shoulder. We were nose to nose, and Dr. Daniels was doing her best to look down on me. Which wasn't a tactic that would work, not with me. "Will, take Pamela down the hallway and get her a candy bar or something."

"Sure."

I didn't turn around, just stood there staring down the doctor. "That kid isn't going anywhere.

I'll sign whatever I need to sign, but you aren't taking her."

Daniels put a finger to my chest and poked hard. "You can't tell me what to do. You are not in charge here. You're just another dumb Yank."

I opened my mouth to speak when a familiar voice cut through the room and chaos broke loose in a most unexpected manner.

"Rylee, help me!"

Spinning, I saw Milly run toward me, her dark brown hair streaming out around her, tears tracking down her cheeks. What the hell was going on? How had she found me here?

She slumped as she reached me, and I barely caught her before she hit the floor, shock making me slow.

Milly was the reason Alex had a death threat on him.

Eve had almost died wearing Milly's spelled anklet.

Giselle had died because Milly had, in a way, forced her to take a truth spell.

"Medic," I yelled, lowering her to the ground, doing what I knew she would expect. Milly still thought we were friends, thought I would help her. Let her think that until the second my sword bit through her spine. Her eyelashes fluttered and she let out a low groan.

I stepped back and eased my swords from their sheaths on my back, holding them loosely at my sides. I didn't have the spell Terese had given me to put Milly to sleep; of course I'd left that at home, not for one second had I thought Milly would find me here in London. Or would want to find me, for that matter. A sudden image of my blood on her moving boxes flashed through my mind. Shit, I'd given her what she needed for a locator spell. They were tough to weave from what I knew, and only worked if you had the blood of the person you wanted to find.

"I'm so sorry, he's gone berserk. I don't know how he followed me here. I didn't know where else to go." She opened her green eyes to stare up at me, looking to me for safety, and my heart clutched against my ribcage, not for her, but for someone else. She couldn't be talking about O'Shea, could she?

No, she wouldn't have tried to take him out too, would she? Shit, of course she would.

Which meant that Giselle's last words meant even more now. *Trust your heart.*

The roar of a man caught between beast and human echoed into the room. Backlit with the light from the open door, O'Shea stood on the threshold, bare-chested, and barefoot with only a pair of tattered khaki pants on, and a flashy gold chain around his neck. A chain that looked remarkably similar to the anklet Milly had made for Eve.

My heart thumped hard at the sight of him, the first in over a month. He'd leaned out, any excess he'd burnt off with the shifting from wolf to man and back again.

"I'm here to kill Alex," he said, the words in a monotone, like a robot working on command. It had to be the collar, there was no other thing that would make O'Shea go after Alex, even at his weakest time when he first was bitten he managed to control himself.

Alex swayed side to side as he clung to a chair, ears flipped back in submission. "Not right, not right. No kill Alex!"

Not taking my eyes off O'Shea, I said, "Milly, hold O'Shea back. Something's wrong and I need to talk to him." I knew she would refuse, but I had to ask.

Her words were soft, and I could hear the regret in them, but she didn't apologize. "I can't, I'm exhausted."

Fuck, I hated being right! O'Shea's eyes flicked over me then skidded over to Alex. With a second roar, he leapt through the room, scattering people as their brains finally clicked in. I heard the first shot of a gun, felt the bullet career past my head, though I was a long ways from O'Shea and the bullet's trajectory.

"Gun's won't work," I yelled, yanking my two blades free of their sheaths. I stood in O'Shea's path.

Time seemed to slow, giving me long moments to think. I didn't want to do this. My heart slammed against my chest and in a moment of desperation, I Tracked O'Shea. Sure, he was right in front of me, but I needed to know what he was feeling.

Anger. Fear. Desperation. Shame.

Shit, this was about to get bad real fast.

"Liam, don't do this!" I knew I somehow had to get to the torc, past his reach; then time seemed to pick back up again. My onetime lover-newbie werewolf and FBI agent slammed into me, knocking me to the floor. Could I have run him through? Yes, but I couldn't, not with what I knew in my gut, in my heart. This wasn't O'Shea; this was Milly. I rolled to my feet. "Alex, here," I yelled, and the werewolf skidded out of O'Shea's reach and cowered behind me.

O'Shea twisted around toward me and the ache in his eyes, the pain there stunned me. "Don't do this," I said, my hand shaking. "I don't want to kill you, Liam!" I had to keep Milly thinking I believed what was going on. Keeping Alex behind me, I pushed backwards, working my way to where Milly had last been.

The Officers in the room were spread out, watching this play out like a hostage situation, which I guess, in a way it was.

The patter of little stocking-covered feet reached my ears, but I couldn't look away from O'Shea.

"Pamela, stay out of the way," I yelled.

"I can help," she said, and O'Shea was lifted into the air, caught in a spell that Milly should have been able to do blindfolded.

I lowered my blades and took in a deep breath, finally looking over at Pamela, "You okay for a second?"

She bobbed her head in agreement and took a bite out of her candy bar. "Yes, I can hold him like this for a long time."

Milly slowly stood up, shaking her head. "I'm so sorry, Rylee. Truly."

"It's not your fault," I said, walking over to her, readying my body for the fast lunge and slice of the blade it would take to remove her head from her shoulders. For some reason, I didn't want her to suffer. Stupid me. "You couldn't have known—" a chair slammed into me from behind, sending me to the ground.

A nightstick was next, and I got bitch-slapped twice with it before I got my hands wrapped around the weapon, effectively killing the magic on it.

I flung the nightstick at her and stood, a sword in my hands.

"Bring it, bitch," I growled.

Eyes wide, she stared at me, shock filtering through her green orbs slowly.

"So, we are on two sides, are we?"

"Have been for a while, I just didn't know it," I said, swirling my two swords, loosening my wrists up.

Sadness etched her features. "This is the only way." She turned to face Pamela, and I felt her gather her power, the black aura around the spell visible even to me. A death spell, one that would eat the kid in a matter of seconds.

"Pamela, get down," I screamed as I launched myself at Milly.

The black spell left Milly's hand as I hit her full-on, tackling her to the ground. Nothing but the pounding of my own heart filled my ears in the moment it took to hit the ground with Milly.

Milly effectively cushioned my fall, though her screech brought sound in living color back to my ears. People rushed around us as if we didn't exist, and I took the moment to look at Milly, to try to discern where things had changed.

"Milly, why?"

She looked away, tears streaming back into her hair "I'm doing this for you, Rylee. I'm trying to keep you safe."

"That makes no sense," I said, my voice hardened. "And it doesn't matter. You've signed your own death warrant."

She looked at me then, her eyes as green as always, but harder than I'd ever seen them.

I moved back enough so that I could jerk her to her feet, keeping her hands clasped in mine and keeping her magic from flowing.

Looking around the precinct, desks and paper were everywhere, and there was a group of officers clustered around where Pamela had stood. My heart sunk until I saw a blonde head bob around the group and walk toward me, blue eyes serious.

"Two of the officers took the angry werewolf to a cell, but I didn't let him go until they got him there."

I licked my lips, then nodded, thinking perhaps it wasn't best that Pamela stay with me. Shit, within hours of meeting me, she had a death spell tossed at her and a rampaging werewolf within ten feet of her. Not a good sign. I had to get the collar off O'Shea, before anything else.

"Aren't you going to introduce us, Rylee?" Milly asked, her voice full of venom.

My mean streak surfaced. "Meet your replacement."

Milly stiffened against my hands. "She won't be able to replace me."

I snorted. "She already has."

13

Milly was placed into a cell despite my protests that she wouldn't be there come morning, and for some reason, no one would let me run her through. Nor would they allow me below in the cells, stating I wasn't cleared, that I could be trying to help Milly and O'Shea. Fuck them all, they'd find out soon enough how very wrong they were to think they could hold a witch behind bars. Everyone scoffed at me. Or at least, every human did. The two other shape shifters, Will and Officer Smith, were guarding O'Shea's cell and keeping an eye on Milly while they were at it. So far, we hadn't been able to get close to Liam. Whatever Milly had done to him with was keeping him raging at anyone who came too close. Pamela said she could hold him so we could remove the collar he wore, but Dr. Daniels was being a major pain in the ass, not allowing Pamela out of her sight.

On that line, Dr. Daniel's used the chaos at the precinct to harp on the fact that an officer had been killed only feet from where Pamela had stood. If only the doctor had understood that Milly had been aiming for Pamela, I had no doubt that the kid would have already been whisked away.

As it was, Agent Valley stepped in, surprising the hell out of me yet again.

"Dr. Daniels, was it?"

The red faced, red dressed doctor nodded sharply. "Yes."

"Agent Adamson," he said, giving me a full title, and I choked as if something had gone down the wrong tube. Agent Valley just gave me a warning look and continued. "Agent Adamson is one of the best agents we have and has dedicated her life to going after cold cases where children have been abducted. If young Pamela wants to stay with her for a short while, I personally will vouch for her safety."

The doctor shook her head. "That is *not* good enough. We have to proceed with the proper procedures and the proper paperwork. This is . . ." Their voices trailed off as Agent Valley herded her away from me, Pamela, and Alex, who sat with his chin on Pamela's knee.

"Pamela, as much as I appreciated your help, this isn't safe for you. The doctor is right about that," I said, slumping into a chair beside her.

"You're going to make me go with her?" She asked, her voice quavering.

"No, I'm not. You have to make up your own mind and I think you're old enough. But my life isn't safe. What you saw just now, that sort of shit happens all the time. You could die if you stay with me." I couldn't pull any punches here, she had to know the truth before she made a decision to stay or not.

Her blue eyes went thoughtful for a moment before she answered. "But you save kids, right? Kids like me?"

I nodded. "Whenever I can."

She bowed her head, her face curtained by her raggedy blond hair. After a moment, she lifted her head; her blue eyes were clear, looking far older than her fourteen years.

"I want to help you," she said. "You need someone like me, someone who can do magic. I want to be her replacement."

Couldn't argue with that. But there was one thing bothering me. "You don't act much like the teenagers I know."

She pulled her bottom lip into her mouth with her teeth, sucking at it before speaking. "My parents kept me locked up from a pretty young age, as soon as I was able to . . . do things."

I closed my eyes and tried not to think about how shitty her childhood had been. We had a case to solve, kids to bring home, and then I could go after Berget. And hopefully somewhere in all of that, I could give Pamela some semblance of a life.

The cell stunk like fear, piss, and vomit, none of it his own; they assailed his now sensitive nose, making him breathe shallowly. The coolness of the lower cells didn't bother him, but the fact that directly across from him sat Milly, did.

Next to his cell stood two shape shifters, one a werewolf like him, and the other—he drew in a deep breath—smelled like a mountain lion he'd caught wind of once.

The cat shifter had tried talking to him, but had given up when O'Shea hadn't been able to answer with anything but snarls and a lunge at the cage. Milly glared at him from across the way. Still, he could do nothing without her explicit command and she hadn't said anything since she'd said, "Kill Alex."

Seeing Rylee had put him into a tailspin, her tri-colored eyes staring up at him, and all he'd been able to say was, "I'm here to kill Alex." Rylee would kill him. She promised him once that if he hurt Alex, she would. And Rylee was, if nothing else, the kind of girl who followed up on her word. Milly had planned this well.

Milly stared hard at him, her lips moving softly as she whispered a command, her eyes flicking to the werewolf. "Kill him."

Without hesitation, O'Shea reached out and snagged the werewolf by the neck through the bars, snapping it with a sharp twist. The cat shifter whirled around and Milly hit him in the back with a spell.

Two more quick incantations and both cell doors were open. Milly flicked her wrist, slamming the cat shifter into the far wall, where he slid down into a crumpled pile.

"Is he dead?"

O'Shea listened, heard the heartbeat steady on the cat shifter. Milly hadn't commanded him to tell the truth.

"Yes."

"Then let's go. We have work to do."

Unable to fight her, O'Shea followed in Milly's wake.

Within five minutes, the sounds of fighting and the feel of heavy-duty magic floated up to us from the lower cells. Fuck it all to Hell and back. Pamela stood, and I put a hand on her shoulder. "No, we wait here." I knew that if I went down to the cells, she'd be right behind me. I couldn't risk her. Not even for O'Shea.

A full minute passed and then another. and finally, Will stumbled up, his head bleeding from a gash. "They're gone."

I nodded, totally unsurprised. There was no real way to keep Milly from using her magic unless I was right there, holding onto her. Officers ran to the lower levels, but I knew they were too late; it had been too late when they put Milly in a cell and expected her to stay there. The humans always took the longest to learn.

Without a doubt, Milly had O'Shea enthralled, of that much I was certain. There was no way he'd have done what he did, not even as a werewolf. His drive to protect others, to do the right thing, would have only intensified as the wolf in him grew. If we'd only been able to get that fucking torc off him.

I helped Will to a chair, gave him a quick once over after pressing a bandage to his head, then stood back. "You're lucky she didn't kill you."

Will lifted tired eyes to mine. "She asked him if I was dead. He lied to her."

I wanted to fist pump. I knew it! "She has him under a spell or something. He's not like this."

"So we shouldn't try and kill him?"

I shook my head.

Will stood up. "Then I better tell the other guys that."

My gut clenched, and I put a hand on his arm. "No, if he comes at them" —I swallowed hard— "he won't hold back. It won't be his fault, but he wouldn't want other people to die just because of what's happened. Not even to save himself."

Will's eyebrows climbed. "You know him that well?" The unasked question, 'You two were a thing?' hovering between us.

I answered both. "Yes."

Will limped off and I leaned on the table, staring down at the paperwork. As if we could catch the Necromancer that way. This was the problem with the human law, with the rules and regulations that choked the life out of those doing the right thing, and allowed the assholes to climb through a loophole made up of paperwork and unjust laws. Looking around, I saw officers putting the office back together, watched them quickly settle back into their seats at their desks. Heads down, fucking heads in the goddamned sand. I knew what we were dealing with, knew that it was a Necromancer, so why weren't we Tracking him, getting this case taken care of? Because someone hadn't signed a sheet of paper giving me the right to go after him? Because the stupid humans thought they were safe behind their file folders and lists of procedures? Fuck this.

Enough was enough.

"Alex, Pamela. We've got to do some Tracking, we've got to end this case now, so we can get on to other things."

Pamela looked up at me, her eyes shrewd. "Like saving that man, that werewolf?"

I touched the top of her head. "Yes." My list just seemed to keep growing, as if someone was actively trying to keep me from going after Berget. It wouldn't surprise me in the least if that was actually the case.

Pamela took Alex's leash and the two of them followed me through the chaotic office and out the front door. Yes, I left without telling anyone, and yes, I took a minor that technically I wasn't guardian of. But shit, when had I ever followed any rules but my own? Besides, not one person even looked up as we left, so mired in their own world that they saw nothing else. Typical humans.

Outside, the crush of fear and swirling emotions subsided, and I locked onto Sophia, the little girl who'd first gone missing. Feeling the pull of her to the north, we headed that way on foot.

"What do you mean we are doing some Tracking?" Pamela asked, her hand buried in the ruff at Alex's neck as we walked.

"It's how I find kids. I was brought here to find a bunch that have gone missing over the last couple of years."

She didn't ask any more questions, seemingly lost in her own thoughts as we wove our way north, avoiding the main roads where possible. At least it wasn't raining now, though the clouds hung low and heavy with the threat of it.

After walking for close to an hour, I stopped and Tracked a second kid, Benjamin. He was in the same direction. From what I could tell, we were maybe another hour away by foot. Really, they hadn't been that far all along. If I'd been here on my own I would have found them within hours of talking to Jack instead of dicking around with reading sheets of papers that did nothing. Okay, to be fair, it was good to know what we were dealing with, but even knowing it was a Necromancer who'd taken the kids didn't change anything. There was nothing different I would do.

Alex was blessedly quiet through the walk, my orders from earlier to keep his mouth shut finally kicking in. Pamela, on the other hand, started up with the questions again.

Why did I have a werewolf for a pet?

Were vampires real?

Who would train her?

Would she be coming back to the States with me? It seemed like once the questions started, the floodgates were opened and she didn't want to stop.

I had a werewolf for a pet because his pack would kill him.

Yes, vampires were real.

A Coven would help with her training *if* she came back to the States with me.

"Am I asking too many questions?" She asked as we crossed the street, merging with the flow of people on the other side.

I shook my head. "No, its fine, but when we start to get closer, we have to focus on the job."

"What do you want me to do?"

"What can you do?"

It turned out that, for an untrained witch, Pamela had learned quite a lot. Spells cast by someone like me, someone who wasn't a witch, always needed an ignition word. But as a witch, Pamela—like all those who were very talented—could spell with her mind and a quick movement of her hand. Once she ran through the list of spells she could manage, I picked a few.

"The spell for lighting up the darkness, can you crank that up so that it's like a burst of light?"

Her footsteps on the pavement faltered, her pale brows furrowed in thought. "Yes, I think so."

"Okay, when we get there I'll give you the go, and you give a good burst of light. Then I can get in, grab our perp and be done with this." It all sounded so good, so easy.

It had to work.

But with a plan, you just never knew if it was going to pan out or not; which was why I loathed to make them.

14

The three of us crouched behind a thick hedge, two houses down from the pristine old Victorian manor where the thrum of the deceased kid's threads beat. Four stories high, the house was beautifully painted in blue with gold and cream accents along the windows and the columns. Stained glass was set in on some of the windows, giving off a splash of color.

"It's very pretty," Pamela said, her eyes wide.

Alex sniffed the air. "Pretty stinky alrighty."

I couldn't smell anything over the greenery we were using for cover.

"You ready?" I looked over at Pamela, who nodded, her fingers clenching one another.

"Yes."

"Okay, let's go. I'm going to make my way onto the front steps. When I get there, you do a blast of light, okay?"

Again, she nodded, blinking rapidly. "What if I can't?"

"You just stay back, that's your job. If you can't give off a burst of light, don't worry about it."

Patting her on the shoulder, I slipped out from behind the hedge and, using what I could for cover, made my way up onto the steps of the Victorian house. The kid's threads were stronger yet, mingling inside my head like a steady pull, drawing me forward. I thought about Milly and her ability to twist threads and make me believe people were alive when they weren't. No, she wasn't in on this case, even if she *was* in London. I knew that much.

Turning ever so slightly, I raised my right hand, giving Pamela the signal and waited with my eyes closed.

Nothing. I peeked back at her and she shook her head.

Okay, going in on my own then. Nothing new here. I had a brief moment of guilt flash through me since Agent Valley had specifically asked that I wait on them. But this was different now; I had to get Liam away from Milly, which meant I had to get this case dealt with. Besides, the FBI and Interpol officers were likely in the middle of something important. Like a donut run. I wouldn't want to disturb their routines.

One hand on the knob of the door, I twisted it carefully, slowly, and felt the door give a little. What bad guy didn't lock their door? Either this idiot was so full of himself he couldn't care . . . or a thought hit me, a rather unpleasant one that only just occurred. He could have a horde of the undead waiting for me. I'd never fought an actual zombie before and wasn't sure what I felt about it, if anything. Like most supernatural creatures, if you remove the head, it was a safe bet you dealt the deathblow.

And if not, burn baby burn.

I stepped across the threshold, felt the slightest tingle of magic slither over my skin, disappearing as it touched me. Score one for the Immune. I closed the door behind me with a soft click.

Creeping into the house, I strained my ears, listening for the sound of anything that would give the Necromancer away. But the place was beyond silent.

Making my way to the stairway, I worked my way up, startled by the first picture I saw. Sophia, the first little girl who'd gone missing; her face relaxed in sleep. Or in her case, likely death.

All the way up the stairwell were pictures of the missing children, all of them with eyes closed, sleeping. Ripples of unease whispered down my spine. What the fuck was this guy into? Was he a pedophile of small dead children? Gods, I hoped not. I couldn't imagine trying to tell any parent that their child's body was used in such a way. Even if they were already dead.

I shook my head to clear the downward spiral of my thoughts. This guy would get his due in a very short while. The second and third floors were clear. Which only left floor number four. As I stepped onto the final landing, the air around me shifted, tensing as if it were a living thing ready to strangle me. Not exactly a comforting image. Across from me was a single door painted in a garish red that seemed out of place with the rest of the house's comforting paint job. The handle on the door was a gold lever, one that wouldn't take much to break if I had to.

The scent of rot and mold lingered in the air, teasing my nose into a wrinkle. Yup, this was the right place. Adrenaline ticked through my bloodstream; close, I was so damn close! I could feel the kids, their threads humming along quite nicely. Perfect. I took a step and the threads seemed to quiver and then . . . fuck . . . they were hundreds of miles to the south!

Confusion and anger propelled me into action and I ran across the landing, slamming my body into the red door and busting it open. Rotting flesh and the smell of death warmed over rolled over me in a wave of disgusting air. Gagging, I dropped to one knee as I took in the room. With no lights on, the shadows that danced and wavered about almost looked human . . . of course, that's when one 'shadow' wobbled out to greet me.

The zombie was a man, my height and extremely old. As in he'd been a zombie a long time. His skin was a mix of grey and green, body fluids oozed out from his mouth past broken and missing teeth. Nasty was an understatement. He let out a classic moan and headed my way. Slowly, but I knew that he wouldn't stop until his orders, whatever they were, were completed. I'd never actually met a zombie before. Giselle had taught me about them, but I'd never had the chance to deal with one until that moment. Lucky me, I know.

"Come on, you snot-dripping rotter. Hurry this the fuck up, I've got things to do." I grabbed my sword handles and slipped the blades free of their sheaths. Swirling them, I loosened up my wrists for the coming impact of half-composted bones and blades.

Another shadow moved, closer to me than the first and a female zombie limped out of the corner. Two, I could handle two no problem—

Make that three. Then all the shadows shifted, and within seconds, I was facing at least twenty zombies, all staring at me like I was a McHappy Meal. This was not good.

The thing was, I couldn't run; I had to cross the Veil wherever the bastard Necromancer did in order to catch him.

I took as deep of a shallow breath as I could with the stench and methane filling the air and went for the closest rotter, removing his head and one arm as I slid close to him. Fuck, the smell was making my eyes water.

The group of zombies moaned as a unit as their buddy hit the floor, a gush of viscera and putrescent fluid washing out across my boots. Seriously, how the hell could anyone live with these things?

I moved through my sword fighting forms, flowing from one lethal blow into the next. Until I was grabbed from behind, hands wrapping themselves around my ankles and yanking hard.

The ground rushed up to meet me and I rolled, slashing out with my swords as I fell. By my count I'd taken out six of the twenty. Only fourteen more to go. Nothing to it.

Right.

The zombie on my feet was chewing on the bottom of my boot, so I ignored him for a moment while I dealt with the hands reaching for me. Lashing out, I whipped my one sword in an arc over my head, rotting arms flopping to the ground beside me. It didn't stop the zombies, but it did give them less to get at me with. A swift kick and my boot chewer got his head crushed. They were so far gone it wasn't going to take much. Then again, they were still—

Teeth slammed into my thigh as one zombie dropped on me mouth first. Arms were missing; teeth were still very much in working order.

"No biting, you little fucker!" I punched the top of his head, my fist going straight through the bone and into the grey mass. The smell that erupted from his skull brought my gorge right up and out.

Puking to one side, I scrambled on all fours between their shambling feet, dragging my swords with me. I had to get my back to the wall—then I could deal with them. At least, that was the plan.

I made it to the wall and pushed myself up, the bite in my leg burning, the taste of vomit on my tongue. There wasn't enough room for both swords to swing easily, but I sure as shit wasn't putting one down. The closest zombie to me was only two feet away and I thrust my sword through his eye, dropping him with minimal effort.

"Come on, let's get this over with." I snarled, dispatching the last of the zombies one right after the other, never letting them get close enough to do any more damage.

Breathing hard, which was difficult in the noxious room, I stared at the bodies littered on the floor, their limbs and skin still twitching and jumping; fluids and rotten blood leaking from them.

"That is disgusting," I said through my teeth. And I damn well had to stay inside the room until I found where the Necromancer crossed the veil.

Stepping gingerly over the still twitching bodies, I searched the room, even using my second sight. Nothing. There wasn't a single sign that there had ever even been a spot where the Veil was crossed. What the fuck was going—

Light bloomed inside the house, so brilliant it blinded me completely. With a yell, I backed up, once more putting my back against the wall.

The light faded from behind my closed lids, but I knew I wouldn't be able to see just yet. Was this the Necromancer coming back? And me blind as a bat with cataracts. I was going to kill the son of a bitch Necromancer the minute I found him.

While I held still, waiting for the afterimages burned in my eyes to fade, something grabbed my boot. I kicked out wildly, the weight and feel of the object lending me to believe it was a zombie's dismembered hand and arm. The fingers dug in, inexorably climbing up my pant leg. I opened my eyes, the images around me fuzzy and dark; indistinct lumps of shadows merged with everything. Fuck, this was a pain in the . . .

The scent of cooking flesh brought my head around, ignoring the hand now climbing up over my shins to my knee.

A crackle of flame reached my ears.

"Ah, shit."

I reached down and grabbed the hand, wrenching it off me and throwing it across the room. Moving carefully, avoiding the bodies as best I could, I worked my way to the door. Out of the darkened room, my eyes adjusted a little more, and the haze of smoke climbing up the stairwell was clearly visible.

A voice barely audible over the crackle of the flames reached me. "Rylee!"

That was Pamela.

"Stay out of here!"

"I'm sorry, I tried to do the light show, but it spilled out more than I could stop—"

"Get out of here, right now!" I hollered, coughing on the last word. With a groan, I stumbled half-blind down the stairway, making it to the third floor where the smoke filled the lower landing. Coughing and hacking, I dropped to the floor where the air was only slightly better. More like a bonfire and less like a house burning down around my ears. I never should have asked Pamela to help, she was untrained and powerful—a deadly combination.

I slithered on my belly down the next set of steps to the second floor, where the smoke was black and thicker than one of Alex's farts. There was no way I'd make it to the first floor. Still on my belly, I could feel the heat through the floorboards from the fire below; the house was going up fast. I worked my way along the wall, eyes burning, lungs aching from the smoke filling them.

My fingertips found the edge of a door and I lifted up just enough to get the doorknob open.

Nope, my luck was gone. The door was locked. Pushing to my feet I snapped my leg in a front kick, breaking the door open. I nearly fell through the doorway, kicking the door shut behind me. The smoke was less in this room and I took a deep breath, coughing hard on the smoke leaving my lungs. Across from me was a stained-glass window. Without a second thought I grabbed a blanket bunched up on the only piece of furniture—a hard-backed rocker—and wrapped my hand in it. Three quick punches and the window was gone, leaving just a few ragged edges. As I went to drop the blanket, but a name etched into it caught my eye.

Sophia.

15

Pamela and Alex swarmed me as I dropped to the ground from the second story window. Rolling to take the velocity and impact out of the fall, I still managed to hit hard enough to knock the wind out of me. Alex bounced in front of me.

"Alex wants to jump!"

"Knock it off, you goof." I grunted, dusting myself off.

Pamela's eyes were wide, brimming with tears.

"I'm so sorry, Rylee. I shouldn't have tried again once you were in there."

I waved her off. "Listen, nobody got hurt. Now let's get the hell out of here before the cavalry shows up."

My eyes still stung from a combination of smoke and light burn, so I had Pamela lead the way, and I kept a hand on Alex's collar; surprisingly he was relatively quiet. I tucked Sophia's blanket under my shirt. When we found her, it was something to wrap her in. I had to believe I would find her and the other kids. But what the Necromancer had pulled, how he'd jumped through the Veil with no trace . . . I had no idea how he'd managed that.

Sirens in the distance drew closer, and before they reached us, I pulled Pamela and Alex into an alleyway. The fire trucks and police cars zipped past us.

"You weren't supposed to go by yourself, were you?" Pamela asked.

"Not really."

"Are you going to get in trouble?"

Shit, this kid had more questions than Alex Trebek.

I peeked out around the edge of the building to make sure the vehicles were all out of sight. "Probably. Won't be the first time, so don't worry about it."

What I wasn't telling her was that it was the first time I'd been involved in burning evidence. That was not going to look good on the old permanent record.

Without further ado, we made it back to my blue suite, an early dusk falling with the heavy cloud cover. There was no way I'd be able to go back to the station without showering and clean clothes. If I could smell the smoke and rotting flesh, there was no way Will would miss it.

Leaving Pamela in the main room with Alex, I stepped into the bathroom, and cranked on the hot water. The bite from the zombie stung like a bitch and was oozing a nice yellow pus. What a fan-fucking-tastic addition to the day.

With the water going full bore, I soaped up, re-hashing what I'd seen. The Necromancer knew how to use the Veil to travel in such a way that I couldn't find the entranceway, he had an undead set of guards to cover his back trail, and now he knew someone was onto him. I had fucked up—royally. There had to be something good that I could squeeze out of this day. Wasn't there?

Smoke and rot washed from my body, bandage and herbal poultice on the bite, and clean clothes on, I was ready to head back to the station. A quick glance in the bathroom mirror showed no cuts or bruises on my face, nothing that would give me away.

My hand was on the doorknob when the soft rumble of a man's voice reached out from the living area. A voice I wanted nothing to do with.

Shit, all I had with me was my big bowie knife; my two swords I'd left in the bedroom, which was adjacent to the bathroom. But if I tried to get them, I would be visible to the main living area and he would see me. Not to mention there was no way I could leave him there with Pamela all alone.

"I can hear your heartbeat escalate, Rylee."

Fuck!

I stepped out of the bathroom and eyed up Faris. The vampire looked the same as the last time I'd seen him; eyes a piercing ice blue, blond hair, and stunning smile with only a whisper of fangs. I had to work at slowing my heart rate, at which Faris gave me a slight nod of acknowledgment. This was so not good in so many ways.

"Pamela." I held out my hand to her and she stepped toward me, but Faris barred the way with his arm. Alex shook where he sat, but his lips were slowly lifting back over his teeth.

"Come now, I was just getting to know the girl," Faris said, reaching out to stroke Pamela's hair. She cringed away from him.

I pulled out the bowie knife. "Let her pass . . ."

He laughed. "Or what, you'll stick me with your butter knife?"

My eyes narrowed; I had nothing to threaten him with, no weapon that would truly hurt him, no blackmail to make him do what I wanted.

"I could use another witch," Faris said. "The one I have is a pain in the ass. And this one is young and teachable . . . malleable."

He spoke like we were business associates out for lunch.

Alex sidled up to me, pressing himself against my legs. "Smells like Milly."

If there had been a light bulb over my head, it would've exploded. Milly had a way to locate me, via my leftover blood, and if she was working for Faris, he had access to that ability. That was singularly disastrous in my mind. If he could find me anywhere . . . it was almost as bad as him being able to Track me.

Only one way to find out if that was the case. I managed to keep my voice even. "Milly's working with you?"

Faris nodded, though his eyes never strayed from Pamela, and I saw her sway. He was enthralling her.

No time to waste, I took two steps toward them and threw my knife, catching Faris along the side of his face and cutting off the rim of his ear.

With a roar, his head snapped around and his eyes all but nailed me to the spot. "You'd dare attack me when I come with terms of peace?"

My jaw clenched and unclenched, fear pooling in my belly. I had no weapon now and nothing close at hand.

I was in deep shit.

"You can't have her. Bad enough you already took Milly from me."

His blood dripped on the floor, leaving a trail as he stalked toward me. "She was already taken by darkness when I found her. You're blind, Tracker, when it comes to those you love. You never see them for what they truly are."

I stepped back for every step forward he took, my mind racing to find a way out of this. A glance over at Pamela showed her sagged against a chair, eyes glazed over. Alex moved with me, his hackles up and a low growl rumbling through his chest.

"No hurt Ryleeee!" He howled as he launched himself at Faris. Even with his teeth and claws bared, the werewolf was knocked aside as if he were a bothersome fly, not a two hundred-pound supernatural. Alex was thrown across the room, his back slamming into the corner of the door frame with a sickening crack of bone. Limp, he fell to the ground and lay there, unmoving.

"You really should be wiser in choosing your friends. They are weak, young, and so easy to turn against you." He smiled and in a flash pinned me against the wall, yanking my wrists above my head, and holding them there with one hand. We'd been here before, him and me. It hadn't ended well.

"Thanks, I needed the stretch," I said, sweat dripping down my sides. I was so fucked, there was no way out, no lifeline I could grab. I couldn't even get my foot up to boot him in the knee. Doran had given me that tidbit and it had, I was sure, saved my life the first time I'd met Faris. But not this time; Faris was working me over very carefully.

Faris continued to smile. "Do you know how vampires share information?"

I tried to swallow; I did, but I had no spit left.

Did it matter that he was going to kill me, then Alex, and put Pamela into some sort of servitude? Yes, it did matter, yet I couldn't stop myself.

"I'm going to go with smoke signal for the win."

"Do you ever learn?"

I did my best to shrug. "Only when I want to."

His lips pulled back from his fangs. "I want to share with you all I know, Rylee. It's a gift, one I do not bestow lightly. Even Milly hasn't gained this honor."

"I'll pass. You go give your cooties to someone else."

Even if he bit me, he couldn't turn me. But I had a bad feeling that it wasn't a bite I was about to get. Faris's tongue flicked out over the tip of his left fang, drawing blood. With an infinite slowness, his head lowered to mine, his one hand held my jaw still, and his body easily kept mine pinned to the wall.

"Relax, Tracker, this will only hurt a little bit," he murmured as his lips covered mine, the taste of coppery sweet blood coating the inside of my mouth. His power washed out over me, and I responded to the heat of his kiss, my mind blank as to why I shouldn't. He let go of my hands, and I didn't push him away, instead twinning my fingers through his hair and pulling him tight against me. The taste of his blood was sweet like honey and I couldn't get enough of it or him. His arousal pressed against my belly and I squirmed, wanting more of what he had, what he was forgotten under the haze of what he was doing to me.

His fingers slid down my arms, taking one hand and shifting it between us, placing it over his hardness, groaning as my fingers clenched on him.

And then the world around me scattered, pain lighting up my nerve endings for a single heartbeat before I was inside his memories.

O'Shea had no fucking idea where he was. London, yes, but other than that his senses had been completely turned around. When they'd reached the carriage, Milly laid a spell on him blocking his sight and hearing. Except for his nose, which kept on picking up the scent of fish, he had nothing to rely on.

His gut still churned from what had happened at the police station. The look on Rylee's face, the fact that he'd charged her and could have killed her if Milly had commanded him too. There had to be a way for him to stop this. He had to believe that he could break this spell or he'd go mad.

Finally a gust of new air washed in and around him; likely Milly had opened the door. Not that he could do anything about it anyway—commanded as he was not to move. Ocean air filled his nostrils followed by a sharp tang of men's sweat, diesel fuel and fish. Lots and lots of fish. They were either on the docks or very close.

With a blinding flash, he could see and hear, the noise of the docks making him cringe—or they would have if he'd been able to move. Yes, they were on the docks, a large boat trimmed in red and black waited directly ahead of them. The *Saint Marie II*.

"Come along, Liam." Milly called over her shoulder as she headed toward the boat.

Come along? Could he circumvent that? He took a step toward her and then one to the side. Yup, he could do this his way. With her back to him, confident in her spell, she couldn't see what he was up to; this might be the only chance he got. Zig-zagging, he tested the limits of what he could do. As long as he went in her general direction, he could go side-to-side. On the far left was a vendor selling wax candles and a thought popped into his head. Would the torc work if his ears were plugged?

He ran hard for the candle maker, feeling the tension of the torc on his neck increase the farther from Milly he got. Literally at the end of his leash, his throat tensed, squeezing shut on his breath.

"Liam!"

Shit, she was on to him. One last heave and he leapt toward the candle maker's stand, sending the entire wares and the shop owner crashing to the ground. Fumbling in the mess, while the shop owner screeched creating a perfect diversion, he grabbed a chunk of soft wax and tucked it into the hole in the waistband of his khakis. It would have to wait for later, but it gave him a bit of hope that perhaps Milly hadn't bested him yet.

There was no way he was going to just lay down and let her win, not with his life, and more importantly, Rylee's on the line.

Faris's memories were not what I expected.

In fact, there was no blood, no gore, no tearing of throats, or even mutilated bodies.

I was at a ball, one of those old school, big fluffed-up dresses kind of balls. Blinking, I stared around me, knowing that I wasn't there, not really. A waltz played in the background, smooth and elegant; it seemed to be keyed to the dancers instead of the other way around. All of the couples who swept past me were vampires, the tilt of their heads, the tips of fangs glimpsed and then gone, showing me clearly what I was looking at. They weren't trying to hide what they were. The thing is, there were only about thirty couples, which meant that every goddamned vampire in the world was attending this soiree.

"I'll be damned," I said, putting my hands on my hips. Faris wanted me to see a ball and some dressed up vampires? Was he trying to prove how civilized he could be?

My feet didn't move, but the view shifted and I was now across the room standing next to Faris. Not the Faris I knew, but one that was dressed up in a puffy shirt with long drooping lace sleeves, knee-high boots with pants tucked in the top, and several over the top bling-bling rings on his fingers. How very Lestat of him. Seeing him like this, I could imagine how easy it would be for him to find his victims. If he wasn't a vampire, I could have acknowledged how good-looking he was. No, that was too tame. Even in his ridiculous clothes, the vamp had "Fuck me, baby" written all over him. His hair was longer, trailing past his shoulders, but tied back with a leather thong. Icy blue eyes took in everything, softening here and there. That took me aback. Then he, Faris the vampire that had been trying to play some twisted wicked game with me, winked at one of the serving ladies. She was quite a bit older, dowdy, and obviously not used to attention from the vamps. She blushed and he gave her a smile.

Well, I'll be damned, he was being . . . nice. I didn't like it. I didn't need my view of him challenged. A hazy feel of lips on mine, and my hand on a hard piece of decidedly male anatomy filtered through me. What was going on with my real body? Shit, this memory had better hurry up.

The music faded and the crowd parted for a matched pair of vampires, a perfect set, thin circlets set on their heads. My guess was these were the previous leaders, the ones who'd been killed by none other than Faris. Emperor and Empress. They drew close to Faris, and so, of course, just as close to me. Even knowing they couldn't see me, I stepped back.

Red hair the color of dried blood flowed down their backs, and dark, almost black eyes regarded Faris with a cool detachment. They were beautiful, stunning, but in a sharp, cruel way that made me want to cringe.

Faris went to one knee, inclining his head ever so slightly. A subtle gasp went around the room. How was I not surprised he would give them offence?

"Faris," the Emperor intoned, his voice rippling out over the crowd amplified right to the point of making you want to cover your ears. "You are being difficult again."

"My liege, never have I been difficult."

The Empress laughed and leaned forward, giving me an ample view down the front of her shirt. Small bite marks marred her creamy skin as far as I could see.

"Nasty," I mumbled and her head snapped up . . . as if she could hear me. I froze in place. Had Faris somehow transported me here? Fuck, I was so dead.

"What is it?" The Emperor asked.

She shook her head, eyes searching where I stood.

"I felt someone, as if they were here, but not. A shadow of a soul." She laughed, soft enough that her lips moved only fractionally. "It feels like the kiss of a lost one."

She might as well have grabbed me around the throat and squeezed. That was what Giselle had called me. Sort of. She'd said I had the Blood of the Lost ones in me. I took a breath, held it, and then let it out slowly. No, they couldn't see me; I wasn't really here. Was I?

The Empress shook her head again, and then looked back to Faris.

"You know the rules, Faris, and you know we have changed them."

"To favor your so-called child."

Again, the gasp went up around the room. I got the feeling no one took on the vampire royalty. Again, how did it not surprise me that Faris was doing just that?

"Yes," the Emperor said, smiling down on the still kneeling Faris. "We would favor her. She is the one the Empress saw, the one who will bring the world to its knees, and put our kind where they belong. Ruling the humans."

I grit my teeth. I didn't like this, not one bit. But I had to admit, at least to myself, that it was fascinating to watch this little drama play out. The tension was building and I knew from experience that something big was coming.

"That is a fool's way," Faris snapped, lifting his head to glare up at his leaders. "We would decimate the population; our kind is not meant to live that way."

There was a subtle shift in the room, a collective stepping back. Everyone was getting out of the way.

Faris straightened his legs and stood, facing the redheaded vampires. "You would go against the very creed?"

The Empress tipped her head and once more looked at me; I squirmed where I stood.

"I believe you are challenging our right to rule. Is that correct, Faris of the muddied blood?"

The vampire I stood beside shivered, his blue eyes going glacial.

"You have no right to dictate." He acted as if she hadn't insulted him. "The Old One is to be asked and then the challenge given. That is the way. That is how we have survived each passing of our liege to the next."

Before the Emperors could respond, Faris lifted his hand, beckoning someone from deep in the shadows of the room.

There was a shuffling behind us and a petite old woman stepped into view. She was ancient, her face a line of wrinkles, yet they were surprisingly pleasant. There was the look of a sweet old granny in her, and I struggled with that thought knowing that she was a vampire, the slightest flash of fang confirming my thought. She was dressed in a floor length grey shimmering gown that was offset by her long train of bright white hair. Her hazel eyes were clear though, sharp in their intelligence. Maybe the sweet old granny analogy wasn't as close as I'd thought.

The Old One came forward, using an ornate walking cane to guide her. Faris stepped back to allow her into the presence of the Emperor and Empress. The Old One did not bow nor scrape. She got right to business.

"I have seen in my visions the coming of a new dawn. Soon your bones will be dust and ashes." Her voice had only a slight tremble to it. I wondered how old of a vampire she was if she *looked and sounded* as old as Yoda.

The Empress put her hand to her chest. "You are not the only one with visions."

"I am the only one with *true* visions," The Old One replied, surprising me with her strength and razor-sharp sudden anger.

Reminder to self, don't piss off the Old One.

She, the Old One, closed her eyes. "A Tracker must be found. One who carries the Blood of the Lost. That will be the deciding factor."

A murmur slid throughout the room, voices raised in questions not quite fully vocalized. But all I could hear was the Old Ones words rattling around my brain.

The vampires were looking for me. Did Faris *know* that I had the Blood of the Lost? Shit, shit, shit! I had to get out of here. Panic spilled upward, and I had to clamp down on the inside of my cheek to keep from babbling that it wasn't me they were looking for. A whole fucking nation of vampires, looking for me. Nope, that was not a good sign toward my longevity.

The Old One lifted her cane again, pointing at Faris. "Whoever binds the Tracker to them will be able to seek out the last of the Blood. These are my words, this is my vision, this is what those who wish to rule must accomplish."

Finally the scene faded, and as I slipped away from Faris's memory, I took one last glance back at the Empress.

Smiling right at me, she blew me a kiss.

16

I came to slowly, confused by the sensations running through my body. Someone was breathing softly on my neck, just below my ear and a pair of well-toned arms held me upright. His hardness pressed between my legs, reminding me of the pleasure I'd been feeling only moments before. My head lolled.

"Liam?"

The arms around me stiffened, then let go, dropping me unceremoniously to the ground. With a grunt, I hit hard, remembering as I rolled what I'd just seen.

And who had been holding me; what had we been doing.

I used my momentum to roll up to my feet, facing Faris. He was glaring at me. I glared right back, embarrassed at how easily I'd fallen under his sway, how my body had responded to his.

"Who the fuck is Liam?"

Wow, he seemed really perturbed by the idea that it wasn't him who'd turned me on. My eyes widened and I shook my head as much to clear the lingering arousal as to deny him.

"No. I'm not going to tell you shit."

He drew himself up and continued to glare at me. I just didn't know what was going on. The first time we'd met, he tried to enthrall me, and then he'd attacked me. Next, he helped me get rid of the demon venom (in a roundabout way), and now he seemed almost jealous of the fact that I hadn't called his name after a minor tryst that my mind had barely been present for.

"What the hell, are you bipolar or something?" I frowned at him. "Can you just make up your mind whether you're going to kill me or . . ." Yeah, didn't want to say that, no need to encourage him to—

"To kill you or . . . what?" He purred, his eyes trapping me. Shit, I'd walked right into this one.

I licked my lips, and his eyes tracked the movement sending my heart into a spiral of out of control thumps that I really didn't want to analyze. "Nothing. Kill me or don't. But no more games." Okay, that sounded good.

Right.

He smiled, and it was the smile he'd given the dowdy servant in his memory. "I think we are just getting started. We got off on the wrong foot. I was working under a certain . . . assumption."

"You need to leave. I have kids to find." I itched to have a blade in my hands; vulnerability ate at me. And I was hoping that I could get him to leave, though I doubted he would do so before he was damn good and ready.

Pamela let out a groan and my eyes shot to her. She was swaying on her feet, gripping the back of the chair. "Rylee, what happened?" Her words were slurred as if she were still partially spelled.

Faris turned toward her.

I did the only thing I could. Two quick steps and I grabbed his arm, yanking him back toward me, our faces not more than a whisper apart. "Leave her alone."

"You reek of fear, Tracker," he murmured. "I like it."

It took everything I had not to start shaking. He could pull me apart like a rag muffin doll if he wanted to. But he didn't, he just lifted a hand and brushed his fingertips along my hairline.

"I'll go for now."

I didn't dare take my eyes from him, as if I could somehow stop him if he tried something. Ha! If only it were that easy. He seemed to hesitate, his lips parting and then he stopped.

"You follow your heart too much. It's a deadly way to be in our world."

Then he was gone, slipping out the front door with hardly a sound. I slumped to my knees, remembered Alex, and stood back up, stumbling to where I'd seen him hit the wall. Even the Guardian we'd faced had not been able to knock Alex down, not like this. The werewolf was at a bad angle, his back clearly broken against the corner of the wall. The wall wasn't looking so good either, but Alex . . . shit. His body was at nearly a ninety-degree angle. Backwards.

Shaking, I crouched next to him. "Hey, buddy, can you hear me?"

He didn't answer but his tail thumped weakly, his body already putting itself back together. He would be okay, even with a broken back, but I had to straighten him out unless I wanted a crippled werewolf at my side for the rest of my life. Goddamn that vampire for making me do this.

"This is going to hurt a minute. But I have to do it," I said. One big breath, and I gripped his hind legs and pulled them out straight, aligning his body, his spine crackling where it had begun to heal.

Alex let out a whimper, and then stilled, blessedly passing out.

I got a blanket and covered him up on the floor. Fuck, he would be sore for at least a couple of days. A spinal injury was the worst thing that could have happened; but at least he was alive. Fuck Faris and his need to show up at the worst possible time.

"You just rest, buddy." There was nothing else for him now but to heal. The rest of the case was going to be on me and me alone.

Next, I moved to Pamela. Her eyes were only at half-mast, her lips drooping. I snapped my fingers in front of her face. Nothing.

"Pamela, wake up." I said, clapping my hands. Again, nothing.

Prompting her, I led her to the kitchen, grabbed a glass and filled it full of water. "Come on, Pamela. I don't want to get you wet, but I will."

I shrugged—wet wasn't all that bad—and flung the large cup of water in her face.

Gasping, her eyes flew open, and the cupboard doors ripped off their hinges and flew into the air as her power pulsed out of her. She spun, crouching as she scanned the room. Good instincts on her, at least.

"He's gone."

"Did you kill him?" She didn't get up from the crouch.

"No, not yet. He's stronger than me by a long shot. If I get a chance, well, that'll be the day I end it for him. Vampires don't give you many chances, though. That's why they're at the top of the food chain."

Pamela shivered, eyes wide with fear. "I couldn't stop myself, I . . . ." She knelt down, her shoulders shaking as she cried out the terror and the guilt. How did I know what she was feeling? Cause I was struggling with the same emotions. Faris just seemed to have that effect on people.

Helping Pamela to her feet, I led her to the bedroom and handed her some of my clothes. "Here, see if these fit."

I went back out and checked on Alex. His big golden eyes were open. "Alex hurts."

Stretching out beside him, I carefully put one arm across his middle. "I know, but it will get better."

"Promise?"

"Promise. But you're going to stay here until you're better."

He didn't answer me, his breathing eased and he slipped back into unconsciousness. Good thing too, since painkillers wouldn't have helped him any, at least no human ones. And I had nothing in my gear for something of this magnitude. What I needed was a Shaman, and I didn't think I was going to find one of those over here in London.

"These fit okay," Pamela said.

Lifting my head, I could only see that the bottom of my jeans had been rolled up at least three times. She was dry and ready to go.

Giving Alex one last stroke across his head, I dusted off my pants. "I'm going to get my weapons, and we need something for you too."

"I have my magic."

I snorted. "How's that working out for you today, again?"

She lowered her head. "I said I was sorry."

Maybe I was being too tough on her, but I knew what Giselle would say. Better that I was tough on her and she survived rather than the alternative.

"Don't be sorry. Just learn. That's your job now. You can't always rely on your magic. You saw how Milly was able to be taken down?" Pamela nodded and I went on. "I didn't even have any weapons."

"So I need to learn to fight, like you?"

"Yes." I handed her two of my blades, each on their own sheaths. "Take these, find a spot on your body where you are comfortable with them."

She fiddled with the leather sheaths and straps for a moment while I put on my crossed back sheath.

"Where do you think I should keep them?"

I took the first one from her and had her turn around. "You right-handed?" She gave me a nod and I went to work. "I like to keep one in my lower back, sideways like this." I laid the sheath perpendicular to her spine, the handle easily reached by her right hand.

"The other one . . ." I motioned for her to lift her left leg and I strapped the smaller blade to her calf. "Lots of people strap their knives too low; all that does is impede your ability to run."

Her blue eyes widened. "Run?"

"From the bad guys."

I finished getting my gear together and then gave Pamela a once over. Bedraggled was the first word that came to mind. Her hair was damp and knotted, her clothes were too big and her eyes too wide. I tentatively Tracked her, getting the gist of her emotions.

Fear was at the top of the list, followed by guilt, and then uncertainty.

The kids were waiting on me, as was O'Shea and Berget.

But Pamela needed me right now. I sat down on the edge of the bed, thinking about what Giselle would do.

"Go in the bathroom and grab my brush and hair elastics, would you?"

She nodded and scampered off. Likely, she thought I was going to show her some wicked way to use a brush to kill someone.

As she came back in, I pointed at the floor in front of me. "Sit; put your back to me."

I took the brush from her hands and worked my way through her tangled hair. Pamela flinched when the brush first touched her scalp, but slowly relaxed as I combed out the snarls and the rats' nests. How long had it been since someone had laid a gentle hand on her? Despite my past, there had been moments of kindness, mostly from Giselle, but even my parents had treated me well before Berget went missing.

"This is nice," Pamela whispered.

The tension in the air Faris had left behind slowly dissipated. Maybe Pamela wasn't the only one who'd needed a moment to breathe. To slow down. I so easily got caught up in the rush of doing what needed to be done, forgetting that not everyone could keep up. Even at times, myself.

Her hair was silken under my hands as I braided it, thinking about Berget and the times I'd braided her hair.

"One or two braids?" I asked.

"Two. Please."

I thought about the picture we made, if anyone had come in. I was decked out in my leather jacket still, the tips of my swords peeking above my head. Pamela sat at my feet playing with the knife we'd strapped to her calf. But still, it was soothing to braid her hair, to let my fingers do something so innocent for once.

Tying off the second braid I patted her on the shoulder. "There, that should be better."

Her hands went to her head, fingers tracing down the bumps of the braid. "Thank you."

"Yeah, no problem. Now let's get going. We've got work to do."

Pamela stood up, faced me, and smiled. Really smiled, and I knew I'd done the right thing. There was my one good thing for the day.

I'd made my new witch smile.

Of course, the smiles didn't last. Not once we'd made our way back to the police station. No, the smiles were wiped off our faces in about three seconds flat.

It started with Denning.

"Who the hell do you think you are? You were seen fleeing from the scene of an ARSON!" He was roaring by the end of his sentence, his face brilliantly red with fury.

Then Agent Valley jumped in on the act. "God damn it! Did I not say wait for us? Are you incapable of following ANY orders?"

Then it was onto Will. He was the worst. He didn't say a word, just ignored me and Pamela as if we weren't even there. I sat in the chair at my desk and Pamela pulled up a chair next to me. I knew a silent treatment when I saw one.

Wouldn't work though, at least not on me.

"Pamela, what did you think of that vampire?" I asked, pointedly not looking at Will.

Her eyes widened and her mouth dropped open, but the girl caught on quick. "He scared the shit out of me."

I reacted the way Giselle would have when I was young. "Language. You can use whatever bad words you want when you're an adult. Not when you're a kid."

She blushed, and I leaned back in my chair, fingers laced behind my head. I Tracked the missing kids, getting a bead on them almost instantly. They were way the fuck out there now, way far south; we'd scared the Necromancer something fierce. Good and bad. He knew we were coming now, but shit, we needed him to hold out, to stick around in one place for a while.

Will finally took the bait. "What vampire?"

"Hmm? Are you talking to us now?" I fluttered my eyelashes at him.

Pamela twiddled her thumbs all innocence and sugar. "I didn't think he liked us anymore," she said softly. Score one for the kid, Will's face drained of color.

"Nah, he's just pissed that we didn't take him with us. Thinks that we should just trust him implicitly though we've known him for less than forty-eight hours." I gave Will a look, the one that had cowed many a man, many a supernatural, for that matter.

It worked like a charm. He let out a sigh. "Listen, you just made our job that much harder—you erased evidence, all those kids' bodies gone."

I shook my head. "You and Denning and Valley are so busy being angry you didn't bother to ask if I learned anything."

Will's eyes widened, bleeding from brown to green. "Did you?"

I nodded and put my feet up on the desk. I had to play this right or we'd never find the kids, not with half the fucking task force tagging along. Sure, I'd made a mistake. I wasn't fucking perfect. But now I had an idea of what we needed to do in order to catch the Necromancer.

"You in or out, Will?"

There were no other words needed. He grimaced and then nodded. "Yeah, I'm in."

"Good, because the first thing I need you to do is find someone who can help us with the Veil. We need to block an exit if we're going to catch this bastard. He can jump through the Veil without leaving a trace behind. I can't stop that, neither can Pamela."

"Block the . . . is that even possible?"

I wasn't positive, but I wasn't going to tell him that. "My Shamans back home could do it. You got anything comparable?"

He frowned. "Yes . . . there is someone I know that should be able to help. But we'll have to get past my Destruction and that could be tricky, they aren't happy with me right now."

I stared at him blankly, and then lifted one finger to stop him as he moved to leave. "I'm sorry. Destruction? Are you in a demolition crew that I don't know about?"

Will laughed. "A group of wild cats is called a Destruction of Cats. Apt, considering just who it's applying to. Try to stay out of trouble until I get back. I need to check it out with my contact first, and I don't want them to get spooked by you."

I laughed and stood as he moved around the desk and headed for the front door.

"You don't think you're going without us, do you?"

Will shrugged, and then snorted softly to himself. "Suit yourself, but not all the cats are as sweet as me."

Touching Pamela lightly on the arm, we headed out after Will. It seemed that London had shown me a lot of the backside of Will, and while it wasn't a bad view, it did nothing for me. Pamela, on the other hand, seemed more than happy with the view we were given.

"He's kinda cute, isn't he?" she said, her voice low.

I had to clamp my teeth hard, remembering at the last instant how fragile young girl's egos could be. In that moment, I missed Giselle more than ever. She would have known what to say, how to handle Pamela so that she wasn't completely fucked up by the time she was an adult. Poor Pamela, all she had was me.

"Yeah, I guess. If you like a scrawny kind of guy."

She giggled into her hand, and I did my best not to roll my eyes. God save me from witches; maybe they were all libido driven? Shit, the only thing I could hope for was that she didn't turn out like Milly.

17

The boat rolled as they crossed the channel, the waves crashing against the sides, sprays of salty water bursting up and over the guardrails where Milly leaned over, heaving her guts out.

O'Shea smiled, or at least tried to. If he thought he could push her over the edge, he would; if he thought he could get close enough to get some of the salt water on his torc, he'd go for that too. As it was, he'd tried to do both several times to no avail. The witch groaned and started to come back up over the railing, then shook her head and heaved again, long dark hair getting caught up in her vomit. The night sky was brilliant overhead, and it was probably the only thing that kept Milly from completely humiliating herself. There just weren't that many people up at this hour.

Only two people came by to check on her, but they both took one look at O'Shea standing guard and skittered away. Milly had told him to stand guard over her—to not move—the last words she'd managed before starting her marathon puke session.

The candlemaker's wax was still secure in his waistband, but that too was out of his reach. Milly hadn't given him leave to do anything other than what he was doing.

Nothing. Just him and his brain scrambling for a way out of this fucking gong show. What he wouldn't give to be just a werewolf . . . he blinked several times, struggled with the fact that he'd actually thought that. Being made a slave by Milly made his previous issues seem . . . trite.

A snap of wind coursed passed him, and he closed his eyes against the movement and moisture it brought with it. That one blink was all it took, and he and Milly were no longer alone.

The figure in front of him was all too familiar. O'Shea remembered clearly the spell the vampire had put on Rylee, how she'd fought him on her own. His muscles tensed, but he could do nothing. But Faris didn't even look at him. As if O'Shea wasn't even there.

"Milly," Faris said, his tone condescending. "If the baby is giving you that much difficulty, we could correct the situation."

She whirled, her face an odd mixture of green and white under the starlight. "Faris, you shouldn't sneak up on me like that. I could have killed you!"

He laughed, the bastard just laughed at her. "Oh, please. Don't be stupid."

Her face went from white and green to just white.

Please let them kill each other.

If only it were that simple. Faris walked to Milly and tucked her arm in his, an old fashioned gesture that forced her to his side. "Come now, let's have a chat, shall we?" They were facing him now, walking his way.

"No, I said I'd help you, it didn't work. I'm free of any obligation," Milly said, her voice gaining confidence as she spoke. O'Shea took it all in, attempting to memorize everything he heard and saw. There was no telling what would be useful later.

Faris smiled down at her, his fangs just peeking out past his lower lip. "Now, what would make you so foolish as to think you can take care of yourself now? Surely not your FBI agent-turned lobotomized wolf over there?"

O'Shea watched in fascination as Milly stiffened. "He wouldn't hurt me, not while I'm pregnant."

Faris' eyebrows lifted. "Really? I think you should ask him—and make sure you tell him to be truthful about it."

O'Shea knew a trap when he felt it tightening around him.

"Liam," Milly said and Faris' eyes snapped wide, staring hard at him.

"Stop. This is . . . Liam?"

Animosity flowed off the vampire; O'Shea could smell the anger and jealousy as if it were a fine bouquet. Fuck, what had he done to piss off the vampire?

Faris stepped close to him and took in a deep breath. "Oh, I see, you aren't *just* a werewolf, are you?"

Liam felt the rage in the pit of his belly bubbling up and he fought to control it. Nothing he could do about it anyway.

They stood like that, toe to toe, nearly nose to nose. The scent of blood and death rolled around the vampire like incense coiling through a room. That wasn't what got his attention though.

The smell of Rylee on Faris's breath lit a rage in him he didn't even try to hold back.

The fury broke up and through the hold Milly had on him; his arms twitched despite the torc. O'Shea wanted nothing more than to rip the smug vampire's head from his shoulders, bathe in his blood, and . . . the images assaulting him stopped him cold. Not that he'd moved more than a twitch, but it was enough.

"I think you should let your" —Faris made air quotes with his fingers— "wolf," then he laughed and went on, "go. I'd like to see what he kind of damage he could do on his own."

Milly made eye contact with O'Shea. "Tell me the truth; would you protect me and the baby from anything?"

He snarled his answer, not caring if it damned him. "No. I'd let whatever monster wanted a piece of you take you and your god forsaken soul to hell along with whatever devil spawn you carry."

She gasped and reeled backwards, a hand to her chest. As if she was truly shocked.

Faris laughed and patted O'Shea on the shoulder. "I think maybe I like you a little more. Agent Wolf." The vampire leaned in and spoke softly. "But you should know, Rylee will be mine."

He lifted blue eyes to his, the depths of them glittering with hatred.

"All of her will be mine."

The rage spilled out of O'Shea, and with it he spoke of his own volition. "We'll see about that."

Will drove us out to the countryside. That was not terribly exciting; thank the gods for small mercies. I slept most of the way, the chatter of Pamela nattering at Will a good bit of background noise. My dreams were disjointed and disturbing. Milly killing Eve, Alex biting Pamela, O'Shea pinioned by stakes. That last jerked me awake with a gasp. I had never been a Dreamer, one of those people who prophesied via their nightmares. No, but that didn't mean I didn't take my dreams seriously. Sometimes they were trying to tell me something.

Like maybe I needed to go after O'Shea first. He wasn't dead, the kids were.

Jack Feen's voice seemed to drift over me. *You made me a promise. Now fucking keep it.*

Yeah, there was that. I did my best to push the dream away and looked around where we were. The rain sleeted sideways and gusts of wind actually pushed the car around on the dirt road. Add that into the dark night and it was a picturesque scene straight out of a horror movie. Fantastic, just what I wanted for night number two in London.

"Are we almost there?" I stretched my arms above my head and felt my spine pop from sleeping hunched over.

"Yes, a few more minutes. Then we walk."

I glanced back outside. I wasn't a prude about weather, shit I lived in North Dakota, so who was I to complain? But this was rain, not dry cold snow. Rain, lots and lots of rain. Lots and lots of wet.

A few minutes later, Will pulled into a, well, I suppose it could be called a turnoff. It looked more like an accidental dip to the right of the road. He was the first one out, Pamela followed, and I sat in the car looking out at the weather. Of course, Will didn't need a flashlight, and we were to just blindly follow him in the dark, out in the woods, in the rain.

The weather wasn't the issue, it was the whole trusting Will thing. I didn't trust him, not fully. Pamela, I trusted her, even though she was a child. But that was just it, she was somewhat easy to read, she hadn't learned yet to hide her emotions even with her tough upbringing. Yet, I'd been wrong about Milly. Was I wrong about Pamela too? Was I wrong to follow Will? I shook off my worries. No, I'd kill him if he made a step wrong. He wouldn't be the first shifter I'd ended.

With teeth grit against the first gust of wind and rain, I stepped out of the car. The rain bitch slapped me, followed by a gust of wind that would make North Dakota proud.

"Let's get this done," I said. Why was it that every freaking Shaman or Shaman-like supernatural lived in the middle of butt-fuck nowhere? Seriously, couldn't they find a nice apartment in town? Just once I'd like to have that as an option. Just damn well once.

Pamela tucked in tight behind Will, and I followed the two of them. From time to time, I saw Will duck his head to speak to Pamela. I kept my eyes and ears open, wondering how exactly this was going to go down. Keeping my head up wasn't easy; the rain was literally running in small rivers down my scalp and into the neck of my jacket. The front of my pants were soaked through, and already, I could feel the slight squish of water in my boots. I'd love to say at least the smell was fresh and refreshing, but it wasn't. There was nothing I could smell over the heavy intrusion of water on my senses.

"If you don't have a Shaman," I said, raising my voice just enough to be heard over the wind. "What do you have?"

Will paused. "A Druid."

I jerked my head up. "Really?" I knew Druids were still around, of course they were. But true Druids, like true psychics, weren't easy to find, nor were they easy to get help from. The other part of the equation was that Druids, well, they weren't known to be shall we say, personable. Every supernatural has their quirks, the things they're known for.

Druids were known for being assholes. Ambiguous, but still assholes.

Earth-powered, ambiguous, hide behind smoke and mirrors, assholes.

Which, combined with my rapier wit, was probably not the best of combinations.

Will paused, turning green eyes toward me. "You must promise to be on your best behavior. Please."

I made a peace sign with my fingers and put them to my temple. "Scouts' honor."

"That isn't how you make the scouts' sign," he grumbled, a visible shiver running down his spine.

"You okay?" Pamela asked, obviously seeing the same thing I was.

He cleared his throat, shook his head, and stepped back from us. "I'll lead, but I have to be in my other form. If we get separated, you need to keep going. I don't think she'll give us another chance to speak with her. She's funny like that."

"Why would we get separated?" Pamela asked softly.

Will put a hand on her head. "My Destruction are the ones who keep the Druids safe. I'm on the outs with them."

"Why?" I asked, not wanting any more politics than we already had.

Will shrugged, or I think he did in the dim light. "It's complicated."

"Fuck, isn't it always."

Will said nothing more and the conversation was over.

I beckoned for Pamela to step back behind me as Will's body hit the ground. I'd never seen a shifter actually shift and the morbid curiosity had me by the throat for a split second.

"Pamela, turn around," I said, as a visible tear in the skin along his face appeared. One hand on her shoulder, I tried to turn her alongside me, facing away from Will.

"I can take it," she said, stiffening beside me.

"It's not about you. Ever think he might not want an audience?"

She relaxed and turned her back; the rip of flesh was obviously painful if the soft groan he let out was any indication.

We stood there, backs turned to a creature that had skin-rending claws attached to all four limbs. It took everything I had not to grab for one of my swords. A soft whuffle, that noise only cats make, brought my head around.

Will was one big-ass kitty. The outline of his feline black body was barely discernible against the darkness around us.

"You do realize that following a black-as-sin cat in the middle of a stormy night isn't going to be easy for us?" I grumbled, irritated by the whole situation. I just wanted to get this over with, to get back to London, find O'Shea and then go after Berget.

"I can make a light," Pamela said, lifting her hand, and I had a vision of the forest burning down around us.

"Wait, you think that's a good idea?" I put my hand on her arm.

"I can do it," she snapped, jerking her arm away from me.

I shrugged. "Okay, but try not to burn the forest down."

Will gave that soft whuffle again several times in a row, almost as if he were laughing.

A bloom of soft pink appeared above Pamela's head. "There," she said. "See, it's not even real fire."

"Hunky dory," I grunted. "Let's go."

Will led, Pamela was in the middle with her pink glow ball, and I trailed behind. The deeper we went into the forest, the more my back itched. Like some bad movie cliché; we were being watched. Most likely by Will's Destruction, if what he was saying was true.

Unable to stand the tension any longer, I loosened up my two swords and slid them noiselessly from their sheaths. It made me feel better to hold the weapons, to know I could use them quickly if need be.

The soft breath of air displaced was the only warning I had. I dropped to my knees and rolled as the creature leapt across me.

"Pamela, get down," I yelled. Everything happened in a blur. Pamela hit the ground with a scream, her pink light going out, but the creature ignored her. It seemed more intent on our guide than anything.

Scrambling to my feet I ran to Pamela's side, and helped her up as the screams of two very large cats echoed around us.

"What do we do?" Pamela gasped out.

"Get your light going again, we'll have to make a run for it."

"What about Will?" She lifted her hand and light blossomed above us, a pure white cluster of what looked like fireflies.

I slid one sword back into its sheath, grabbed her arm and ran deeper into the forest. "He can take care of himself and he told us we had to book it, so let's go."

"The lorry's the other way."

"But the Druid is this way." And above all else, we were going to meet with the Druid. One way or another.

18

Pamela and I were totally and completely turned around. Lost didn't even begin to cover what we were. I briefly Tracked Will. He was way behind us and going farther away. My gut feeling was that he led the other cat farther from us to give us a chance. The thing was, I had no way to find the Druid on my own, and fuck me, we couldn't even find our way back to the damn 'lorry.'

We were crouched in a cluster of trees, the rain seemingly not inclined to ease up, not even for a second. I wiped my face, wishing for a warm fire and some dry clothes.

Beside me, Pamela shivered violently. I'd already given her my jacket and that had helped, but now that we weren't moving it was harder to keep warm.

"How . . . long . . . are we going . . . to stay . . . out for?" Pamela's teeth chattered and even in the dim light I could see how little color her face and lips had.

Through the downpour of rain, the trees were becoming visible, highlighted at the tops from the slowly rising sun.

"Not much longer. As soon as it's light out we can get moving. Can you hang on till then?"

She nodded and hunkered down deeper inside my jacket. My t-shirt was soaked through and my skin was bumpy with gooseflesh. But I'd survive. I was loathe to give up, but without being able to Track the Druid, I had no idea how I'd find her.

I closed my eyes and tried to think happy thoughts. There weren't many of them.

Jack Feen's words drifted slowly back to me . . .

You can Track groups of people, groups of supernaturals. It's why the vampires want you.

My eyes snapped open. And if I could use that now? Maybe I could find the Druid on my own.

I wasn't sure how to start other than the way I would with a child. Druids were assholes, notoriously difficult to deal with, went out of their way to be hermit-like, secretive. I let the traits I knew them to have coalesce inside my mind, creating a 'picture' of what a Druid should be.

My Tracking ability seemed to hover over the created picture and then with a crack of what felt like lightning through my mind, I could feel the Druid as clearly as if I'd had a picture.

"Bingo." I stood, my body stiff from sitting crouched under the trees for several hours. "Come on, Pamela, I think I've found us a way out of here."

She didn't argue, just got groggily to her feet, slipping her fingers into my belt loop. "I don't think I can make a light," she said.

"Don't need one." I answered, striding off in the direction of the Druid. Different than Tracking someone I had a picture and a name of; in some ways, this was clearer, cleaner. The sense of 'what' the Druid was hummed inside my head, yet I had no definite emotions or feelings. I couldn't tell if the Druid was happy or sad, alive or dead. In its own way, this kind of Tracking was far easier. Or, at least, less emotional. The downside was I suspected it could be any Druid, not necessarily the one we were looking for.

We made our way through a thin patch of trees, over an easily jumpable creek, up the embankment, and then we were looking down on a bare field. I guess there was a part of me that figured we were going to stumble on Stonehenge. Of course, if it were that easy to find a real Druid, the humans would have done it long ago.

The creek we'd hopped coursed out through the bare field, dividing it in half completely and as we watched, the sun rose, highlighting the other niceties of the place. Like the dozen Druids kneeling around an altar.

"I don't want to go down there," Pamela said, her voice full of fear. No doubt the altar brought back memories of the priests.

"Good, cause I want you to stay here." I looked around. "Actually, I want you to climb that tree and wait for me or Will. Got it?"

Her blue eyes, so old for her years lifted to mine. "And if neither of you come?"

Shit, that was a good question.

"Wait till they" —I pointed at the group below us— "are all gone. Then do your best to track your way back to the road."

She nodded, and I boosted her into the lower branches of the tree. At a distance, no one would even see her wearing my leather jacket and dark jeans. Only her hair would stand out, but there was nothing to do for that now.

I only held one sword, the other still strapped to my back, the leather ties squeaking in protest with the wet.

Keeping my gait easy, I sauntered down the slope and walked toward the still kneeling group of Druids.

Doing a quick count, I saw that there were thirteen, not an even dozen as my first glance over had shown me. They were wearing light grey robes with hoods that came up and over their heads, draping down past their eyes almost to their mouths. No point in trying to surprise them, at least one of them knew we were coming. Or at least, I assumed one of them did.

I stopped about fifteen feet away from the kneeling group, put the tip of my sword into the ground and leaned on it. "Hey, which one of you knows Will?"

There was a nice overall stiffening, as the group shifted to stare at me, one at a time from under their hoods. I stared right back. Druids, for all their assholeness, were not generally prone to violence or death magic.

I truly hoped my foggy recollections of them were correct.

One Druid stood and even with the loose hanging robe I could see she was a woman. A ridiculously well endowed, large woman.

She flipped her hood back and my jaw dropped. The lady in red, the woman who'd been trying to take Pamela from me and put her in foster care, was a gods be damned Druid.

"Dr. Daniels, I presume?" I gave her a salute.

"Truly, you have a knack for causing grief, Tracker," she snapped. "If you'd allow me to take the child, she'd already be in training."

"She isn't a Druid."

Dr. Daniels drew herself up, her bosom heaving. "She could be. We could train her."

I smiled and laughed in her face. "Please, with what skills? I'm going to take her back to the States with me where a *Coven* will train her properly." I actually only had begun to formulate that part of things, but no need for them to know it.

Her eyes flashed. "She belongs here, with us."

Holding up my hands in mock surrender, I did my best to curb my tongue, but failed miserably. "Listen, you are a serious pain in my ass, don't tell me that you are the one familiar with Will?" It seemed obvious that she was, but then why didn't he just phone her, or better yet, call her down to the police station?

A second Druid stood. "Familiar would be the correct word, useless Tracker."

Ah, here we go, someone to spar with.

"Useless? This from a bunch of bathrobe wearing" —I stepped forward, leaving my sword where it was— "overweight" —there was a gasp from the group— "child-thieving douchebags?"

All of the Druids stood up and the tension rose with them.

"I'm here to speak with one Druid. The one who knows Will the best." Gods, I seriously hoped it wasn't Daniels.

Finally, there was movement from the back of the group, and a slender Druid stepped forward, flipping back her hood and baring her face to the rain. Strawberry-blonde hair, and seriously pissed hazel eyes tried to pin me down. She was pretty, but there was something familiar about her . . . her lips twisted downward in a sharp line and my eyebrows went up.

"Fuck me, you're Will's sister, aren't you?"

Her frown deepened and with it, so did the likeness. All I could think was that I was so glad I didn't have to deal with Dr. Daniels.

"I am his sister. Where is my wayward brother? He said he was bringing you in and I've been waiting all night."

I glanced past her to the other Druids. "You sure you want to talk about this in front of them?"

Will's sister flushed to the edge of her hairline. "They are my family. I hide nothing from them."

I shrugged. "He was attacked by another cat and drew it away from us." I Tracked him, felt him slowly making his way closer to us. He was hurt, but his life wasn't draining away. "He's on his way now."

The Druids shifted, and then Dr. Daniels stepped forward. "I told you Will was not welcome here."

Will's sister's spine seemed to snap straight as she whirled on Dr. Daniels. "And I told you repeatedly that you are an initiate. You are to speak when spoken to and otherwise—shut the fuck up!"

Nice, at least I wasn't the only potty mouth around here.

Dr. Daniels fell back, did an awkward curtsey and turned away, as if by giving us her back she was giving us privacy.

I didn't want to wait for Will, couldn't if we wanted to get this case over with. "We need your services."

"For what?"

"To help block access to the Veil."

There was a moment of silence, then. "And why do you think I, we, can help you with that?"

Competition is key in any group, and supernaturals, no less. "Well, I'd get one of my Shamans to do it, no problem. They're tough like that. But they're across the water and Will thought *maybe* you might be able to help. He wasn't sure you had the skills, but figured we could at least ask."

Will's sister pursed her lips. "I don't like you."

"Feeling's mutual."

"Give me a reason, a real reason, to help you."

This was where it got tricky. Being so ambiguous, Druids just didn't step out of their comfort zones. Ever.

"I'm Tracking a Necromancer who's been stealing dead, and close to dead, children, and using them for his own purposes. . . ." I didn't know what exactly he, the Necromancer, had been using the children for, but I would let her mind fill in the blank.

Several heartbeats passed, and with each one, her face paled a little more. "Children, used for his own pleasure. . . ." It seemed she didn't want to name it, either.

I nodded and she shook her head slightly.

She touched her fingers to her throat. "My name is Deanna. I will help you."

There was an immediate shuffling of the Druids and again, Dr. Daniels stepped forward.

"Deanna, you can't help her."

Will's sister spun on the initiate, and I didn't even try to hide my grin.

"Penance is what you'll be doing for the next month. Now go!" Deanna's back was to me, but by the look on Dr. Daniels' face, this was a first.

"Penance?" She queried.

The power struggle was an almost visible thing. Druids moved either to back Deanna or Dr. Daniels. What the hell had I stepped into this time?

Deanna had five Druids behind her; Dr. Daniels had six. Damn, this was not looking good.

"I'm not doing anymore bowing and scraping to you," Dr. Daniels said, her voice full of self-confidence. "I will be the leader now. Not you. There will be no penance on my shoulders."

I cleared my throat. "You know, Deanna has already agreed to help me. So I'll just take her with me and go."

Dr. Daniels laughed, throwing her head back in an over-the-top move that just made me want to roll my eyes. What a twat.

Flicking my sword into the air, I strolled into the middle, right smack between the two groups of Druids. "Listen, I'm going to make this easy. Deanna is in charge right now. She's going to stay that way until she gets back from helping me and these kids. You know how I know that?"

A glance at Deanna and then Dr. Daniel's showed me their combined confusion. Dr. Daniels, who piped up, her attitude once again clearly showing.

"You don't know anything of the sort," she snorted, a dribble of snot escaping from her nose.

Grimacing, I lifted my sword up and pointed it at her right shoulder. "I foresee you spending some time in the hospital. That should eat up the whole who's in charge business for at least a day or two. Long enough for me."

"You wouldn't!" Dr. Daniels screeched, but I'd already lunged forward, slicing through the meat of her shoulder, feeling her clavicle separate around my blade. She fell and my sword slid out easily. Blood spurted from the wound, quickly washing into the mud under our feet. The Druids around Dr. Daniels flew into action, lifting her up and carrying her away from us. Her screeching could be heard even over the occasional clap of thunder. The woman had lungs; I'd give her that.

Deanna glared at me. "You make me look weak."

I wiped off my blade and slid it back into its sheath. The straps were stretching with the rain and the fit was getting sloppy. I was going to have to look into some new harness for my gear at this rate. "I make you look like you have a crazy bitch on your side. Not a bad thing in this case."

She opened her mouth as if to argue, then snapped it shut.

With a few murmured words too low for me to hear, she sent her people away, and then moved to my side. "Come, let us get this done. You have bought me time, but not much."

"Lead the way."

With a huff, she strode up the embankment toward the tree where I'd left Pamela. We reached the base and the kid climbed down without having to be told. "Is she going to help us?" She pointed at Deanna.

"Yes, and if I remember correctly, it's rude to point. So only do it if you want to insult someone," I said.

Pamela nodded, her face a mask of sincerity. Shit, I was going to have to be very careful about teaching her bad habits. Then again, Giselle had said she'd given me a bunch of her own.

Deanna led us back through the sodden, mud-filled, rain-drenched forest with ease. She was obviously comfortable here, and while I wanted to ask her questions, I also had the feeling that it wouldn't take much to send her back to her Druids. Which meant I had to play nice.

This was not going to be easy.

19

Back at the 'lorry,' as Pamela insisted on calling the car, Will waited for us. Though waited would make you think he was conscious. He most definitely was not.

Slumped over the hood of the car, blood trickled from one ear and a rake of claw marks bisected his bare back and ass.

I ran forward, Deanna and Pamela right behind. "Will. What the hell happened?"

He groaned and lifted his head. His eyes were purpled shut, lips were swollen, and it pretty much looked like he'd been shit out of a Harpy from a thousand feet up.

"The Destruction was waiting for me. That bitch Daniels knew we were coming. Must have overheard me on the phone at the station."

Ah, that explained that. One more strike against the good doctor. Next time I'd be aiming for the left side.

I helped him to his feet and Deanna came close, laying her hands on either side of his face.

"Brother. This is not good."

"Nothing we can do about it now," he slurred out, groaning as we helped him into the back of the car, covering him with a blanket from the trunk. Pamela climbed in and pillowed his head in her lap. She was crying silently, her tears streaking down her mud-flecked face. Fuck, this had been some night. Certainly not one to put in the memento books.

Deanna didn't drive, so that left me with the task of managing everything that was ass backwards. We drove into town with no problems though, and went straight to my suite, though Deanna argued against it.

"He has medical equipment at his home."

"I have a werewolf I need to check on," I said, pulling into the narrow driveway. Will leaned on me and I helped him into the blue suite, cringing once more at the sight of the gaudy decoration.

"Pamela, go shower and change clothes," I said, and she reluctantly left us. I lowered Will onto the couch as carefully as I could. Deanna stood frozen in the doorway. "You coming in?"

"It feels as though a great darkness has been here."

"Ah, shit, that's the vampire you're picking up on." I grunted, throwing another blanket over Will.

"I have more clothes in the trunk."

I nodded and stood to go get them when I realized that there had been no answer to my vampire comment and looked to where Deanna had stood. She was not in the doorway, or any other part of the suite, for that matter. I ran, opened the door and looked down the street, seeing her walking swiftly away. The bitch was leaving!

"Hey, where the fuck do you think you're going?"

She glanced back and shook her head. I knew what would stop her—something that would stop a Shaman in their tracks too.

"Oath breaker!"

If she had brakes, I might as well have slammed a brick onto them. She stopped so hard and fast, her upper body actually tipped forward.

"What did you call me?"

People on the street were staring, but I didn't care. What the hell did it matter to me if a human got a glimpse of the supernatural? They'd just write it off as some trick of the eye anyway.

"You heard me. You made a promise to help me, to help those kids. And now you're running away. Oath breaker is the least of the names I could come up with."

Deanna stood there, rain pounding down around her, but the weather still didn't seem to touch her or her grey robe. Nice perk.

Finally, she turned and walked back toward me.

I let out a soft breath. If I didn't have her help, I wasn't sure I could nail down this bastard on my own. He was too fast at using the Veil to get away, too slippery, not to mention the whole zombie guard business.

"I do not want to deal with a vampire."

"You won't. He just wants me."

Deanna stepped back inside the suite and I closed the door on the rain, though the sound of it still echoed through the house.

She went to her brother's side; I went in the other room and got the medical supplies I had.

"Here." I handed the kit to her, then went to check on Alex. He had moved, making his way into my bedroom, then to the far side of the room. Curled up in a ball, his face was buried under his bushy tail and he breathed deeply, the sleep of a body healing. The shower was running full tilt and I could just hear Pamela humming to herself.

At least my two charges were alive and well. Now came the tough part.

Back in the kitchen, I went and pulled a chair out for myself. I had to phone Agent Valley and get him up to speed. The suite didn't have a rotary phone, which meant I either went outside to find a phone booth, or I walked down to the station to face Agent Valley in person. Neither option was all that appealing.

Deanna was sitting beside Will, working on his back, cleaning out the claw marks. They were healing, I could see the difference already, but it was always good to get the worst of the foreign bodies out.

A soft pad of big feet snapped my head up. Alex limped out to me and put his head on my knee. "Alex come with Rylee."

His golden eyes were tight with pain, his body was still badly injured and yet, his loyalty won over everything else. A suspicious lump in my throat rose and I fought it back down. This was no time for tears.

With a wave, I got Deanna's attention. "Throw me the kit." She closed the lid and tossed it across the room to me. I opened it on the table and picked out an herbal concoction that dulled pain. It might actually have an effect now that he was not in and out of consciousness. The mix also tended to dull the ability to think clearly, but with Alex, I was less worried about that than I would be with anyone else.

"Open up," I said. I knew then how badly he was hurt. In the past, Alex fought taking any kind of supplement or herbs. Like a child, he would spit and pout and hold his breath. But this time he just opened his mouth and let me pour the sluggish contents down his throat.

He gacked, heaved, shook his head, and then settled back against my leg. For now, it was the best I could do.

"Deanna." She lifted her head.

"Yes?"

"I'm going out. I'll take Alex and Pamela with me, we won't be long."

She was already shaking her head. "What if the vampire comes back?"

I shrugged. "Take a message for me."

Bundling Pamela into the last of my dry, clean clothes and letting her wear my leather jacket, we headed back out into the weather toward the station. Alex was slow, and I eased my usual stride so he could keep up.

"Rylee, will he be okay?" She didn't need to say who 'he' was.

"Will is a shifter. He'll be fine," I said as we turned the corner. We were only a few minutes away from the station and I could already see the grey exterior. And the flood of cops spewing out of it.

I put a hand out, barring Pamela from stepping ahead.

"What is it?" she whispered, immediately picking up on my tension.

Alex lifted his head and sniffed the air. "Stinkers."

The flood of officers out of the station eased off, and then came a new—or should I say old and rotting—mess of bodies piling after them.

Hundreds of 'stinkers,' as Alex put it, poured out of the main doors, grabbing and biting anything close enough for them. The cops fired into the horde, but the bullets swerved and dodged, sometimes swinging back. Fuck, when would they ever learn?

"Stay with me, no matter what," I said, jogging toward the zombies. When I was close enough for the officers to hear me, I yelled out over the screams. "Guns won't work, you morons! Swords, knives, but no ever-loving guns!"

A few listened, but the tide of flesh wasn't really stemmed. Distantly, I wondered how the FBI and Interpol would spin this catastrophe to the public. Then all thoughts flew from my head as I made my first swing with my sword, slicing a zombie in half with a wet crunch of bone and gristle. The smell of rotting flesh intensified, sharp and lingering along my nasal passages.

Pamela retched behind me.

"Stay with me," I said.

Alex let out a growl and a zombie coming in fast on my right went down in a flurry of teeth and snarls. For a submissive werewolf, he'd come a long way.

Swing after swing of my swords and the snatch-and-decapitate technique Alex was employing brought us to the main doors. A peek inside showed that while there were still zombies, there weren't as many. Maybe thirty in the main room, not too bad at all. I used the back of my hand to wipe my forehead.

Pamela pointed. "They're coming up the stairs."

So they were. What kind of game was the Necromancer playing now?

A flicker of movement and the sense that someone was behind me was the only warning I got. I tried to dodge out of the zombie's hands, but he was a big bastard, with mitts almost as big as Alex's paws—mitts that pinned my arms to my sides, making my swords pretty much useless.

"Get the fuck off me!" I flung my body to the side and jerked him off balance, but he didn't let go, not even an inch.

"You will leave my master alone," he slurred out, his voice a drunken monotone.

I froze, pulled myself together, and answered. "Nope, not until he stops taking kids. He's a perverted freak of nature."

The zombie roared, and I knew that the Necromancer was hearing what I said. Good.

"I'm coming for you asshole!" My blood surged, adrenaline pounding through my body even if my arms were pinned. I kicked at the zombie, taking out one of his knees. A second kick blasted out the other kneecap, jagged edges of bone poking out of the ripped flesh. Still he hung on.

The zombie reared back and then his head shot forward, teeth slamming into my lower back just above my hip. Without my leather jacket, he burrowed his face into my flesh like a dog with a bone. The bite and the force behind it sent us both stumbling in through the main doors.

I couldn't stop the scream that ripped out of me. Alex tackled the big zombie, but the rotter's teeth were still in me; a hunk of skin and flesh went with the creature. Snarling and twisting, Alex tore the zombie's head off. I was on my hands and knees, shaking with pain; a quick glance back at my hip made me turn my head away.

The wound was bad. Blood poured out and down my leg, and around my belly. The remaining zombies paused what they were doing and lifted their heads. That much is true about rotters—they love the smell of fresh blood. Like a school of dumb sharks, blood drew them as nothing else would.

I was so fucked.

"Pamela, you need to stop them." I fumbled to get my shirt off. I had to stuff the bite wound with something, anything to staunch the flow of blood. The straps from my sword sheaths got in my way and I fought with them, panicking.

Pale, Pamela nodded, then whipped her arms outward, flicking all ten fingers. The remaining zombies flew backwards faster than I could blink and smashed against the concrete walls. Pinned there with her magic, they groaned and mumbled, but didn't fight overly much.

Standing, I locked my knees to keep from tumbling over. This was a bad injury, the zombie must have hit an artery because I was feeling rather faint . . . that was the last thought I had as the room swirled and the darkness claimed me.

Of course, it was just my luck it wasn't a blissful, quiet darkness. No . . . I had to open my eyes to see Faris leaning over me.

"Zombies? Really, so cliché," he said, smiling like it was a joke that I should get.

Whatever. "Tell that to the Necromancer," I grunted, pushing him away, my hand flat against his chest. Instead, he put his hand over mine and yanked me to my feet, still hanging onto me.

It briefly crossed my mind that every time I ran into Faris, or more accurately, he ran into me, I was less afraid of him. That probably wasn't a good thing that I was getting comfortable with the vampire. No, definitely not a good thing at all.

He continued to hold my hand, and softened his voice. "I need your help, Rylee. You saw my memory. You see what I'm up against. I want to keep the vampire nation as it is. Out of sight. As it should be."

I pulled at my hand, but he only tightened his grip. "Yeah, I saw what you saw. But memories can be tricky. It's all about perception."

"And what is your perception of me?" One finger trailed along the top of my hand, down around to the underside of my wrist and back up again.

I refused to acknowledge the more than pleasant tingle it gave me. Fucking refused.

It took everything I had to keep my heart rate under control. "That you are a master manipulator. Like all vampires."

His eyebrows went up. "All vampires? And how many of us have you met?"

I shrugged. "Doesn't matter, it's the same thing as any other species in the supernatural world. We have our quirks, each of us. Vampires are manipulators, that's a given. It's how I'd Track them if I had to."

Faris's eyes narrowed. "How enlightening."

Oh shit, I should never have opened my big fat mouth. Faris hadn't known I could Track more than individuals. I shook my head in an effort to cover my big ass blunder. "Just pointing out the obvious." But my heart betrayed me, thrumming like it was in a freaking rock band.

The vampire smiled at me. "I'm glad Jack Feen is teaching you. I need you at your best. Which, I suppose, must mean that I need to heal up that nasty bite for you."

Before I could protest, his free hand slipped around my waist, covering my hip where the bite was on my physical body. That wasn't too bad. But the moment his lips covered mine and the little groan of pleasure slipped out of my mouth, horror hit me.

I was willingly kissing a vampire when I was in love with Liam.

Faris jerked back as if I'd stung him. "You would think of him, while I kiss you?"

The rage was not expected. Nor was what he said next as he strode away into the darkness.

"She is mine, wolf. One way or another. Rylee is mine."

20

I shot straight up, gasping for air as if I'd been—

Pamela grabbed me in a fierce hug. "You weren't breathing, there was so much blood."

Everything around me moved as if on high speed, people rushing, paper crinkling, all my senses were in overdrive. The scent of blood and rot overwhelmed my nose and I covered my face. I knew I had to get up and move, this was—

I was standing. How the hell had that happened? Chills swept through me and the taste of Faris' kiss trickled through my mouth. Fuck, he'd imprinted me.

Pamela was talking to me, tugging on my arm, Alex stared at me, his eyes wide and worried. All I could hear was the beat of their respective hearts. Pamela's was wild and erratic in her fear, Alex's beat slow as his body continued to heal as best it could.

"Just give me a minute," I said, waving them off. The zombie situation was more or less under control; however long I'd been out had been enough for the cops to get their asses in gear.

It took an effort to walk slowly, to make my legs move at a normal pace. From what I understood, this would last a short time—how short I didn't know for sure. And then it would fade and I'd be back to my regular self, whenever the hell that was going to be.

The bathroom was empty but for one zombie who I promptly slid my sword through, removing its head with a slurping pop. I leaned against the sink and stared into the mirror, watching my breath fog it up. My eyes were still my own, a swirl of chocolate, emerald, and gold.

Imprinting was how vampires bound their subjects to them. Blood on blood was how it was done, and it was the first step in making someone a vampire. Which meant the vampire's bite was like a poison, something my Immunity blocked. As I stared into the mirror, my hearing settled down, the smells I shouldn't have been able to smell faded.

Fuck me, I'd thought I was in trouble for a minute. I pulled the edge of my shirt down and traced the black snowflake etched into my skin on my chest bone. Demon venom had nearly done me in, the first time my Immunity hadn't protected me completely. Mind you, I'd been able to keep the world from spiraling into an ice age, so I suppose that was something. But the thought that my Immunity wasn't up to snuff again . . . I wasn't sure I liked that. So it was a relief to feel the imprinting fade and slowly slough off.

Letting out a deep, shaky breath, I turned and made my way back to the main room. Pamela and Alex sat where my desk had been. The whole place looked like a typhoon had ripped through, followed by a Giant on a mating quest. Nothing was left untouched, people included.

There were a few officers that had been bitten, and I could see it in their faces, the fear that they would be turned into zombies.

"Oh, get the fuck over it," I snapped. "You watch too many stupid B-rated movies and you think you understand the supernatural? Fuck. You have to be DEAD to become a zombie."

I shook my head as I walked through the room. "What a bunch of idiots." I looked over the different zombies. Male, female, the only thing was there were no kids, just adults. All of them were way far gone, like they'd been zombies for a long time. Maybe the Necromancer was hoarding zombies. I gave a full body shiver at the thought.

On the far side of the room the one who'd grabbed and bitten me was still twitching; they'd do that for hours even with their heads lopped off. Kind of like chickens.

I put a hand on Pamela's shoulder. "You did good. Are you okay?"

She nodded. "Yes, but . . . I heard the police. They said that these were people once."

My eyes closed of their own volition as I tried to put this as delicately as possible. She was, after all, a kid still.

"Yeah, once. But not anymore. Whatever made them human fled when they died and then were raised by the Necromancer."

Her blonde eyebrows dipped in consternation. "You mean it's okay to kill them?"

"Yup. I'm going to encourage it. It's good practice." I was about to do something that any parent organization, foster care system, and every god damn therapist would have been screaming about. I slid my sword from its sheath off my back.

"Here, take this." I handed it to Pamela, who took it awkwardly, her eyes widening.

"What do I need this for?"

I pulled the other sword, walked over to the closest zombie and did the most basic of slashes, removing its left arm. I lifted my eyes to hers.

"Practice. Go around, cut off all the limbs and heads you can. Before every slash, check to make sure there is no one close to you."

She caught her lower lip in her teeth and I saw her pull her back straight. One day she would be strong enough to live in this world. If I could keep her alive.

Agent Valley came stomping in about the time that Pamela took off her first limb. With a squeal of excitement, she spun toward me, gore sliding down the blade.

"I got it!"

"Good job, now keep going."

With a wide smile on her face, she gave me a thumbs up.

"But keep your mouth shut, zombies taste like shit."

Her lips clamped together, but her eyes sparkled. That was just another difference between humans and supernaturals. We thrived on magic, weapons and blood; it was in our essence.

The FBI agent stood in front of me, and I pointedly ignored him, watching Pamela as she hacked away.

"She's making a bigger mess than we need," he said.

"She's got good natural movement. One day she'll kick my ass with a sword if she keeps up the practice."

Agent Valley grabbed my shoulder, his fingers gripping hard, pinching a nerve.

"Is this a game to you? You run off with one of the officers, kidnap a foster kid while you're at it, and then to top it off, you piss off some Necromancer so badly he sends a small army to wipe us out via our own basement?" He wasn't yelling; his voice was soft and intense.

I gave him my best bitch eyes. "Let go of my arm before I have Pamela remove it for you." His hand slowly dropped, and I dusted off my shoulder. "It's not a game. But until you realize that things can't be done within the confines of your rules, things will seem out of control and I won't tell you what's going on."

Jaw flexing, that telltale vein throbbed along his neck. "You need to catch this bastard. Now."

"Are you giving me free rein?"

Boy, I couldn't wait to hear his answer.

He struggled, his facial muscles twitching, hands giving a slight tremor. Finally, he managed to say it. "You have free rein. Take who you need, but make it fast. Interpol isn't happy with you—"

"Well, there's a surprise," I muttered.

"And they want you gone. As in yesterday. They think they have enough information to take this guy down themselves."

There was a commotion at the door and we stopped talking to stare as Will limped in, aided by his sister.

"Feels a bit like a bad joke," I said. "A shape shifter and Druid walk into a police station recently molested by zombies."

Agent Valley snorted. "You forgot the part about the witch child hacking off zombie limbs with a sword."

I leaned back and laughed. "You have potential, Agent Valley. This is my life. Welcome to it."

He stepped closer to me, his face serious. "What do you need to make this happen?"

Lips tight, I dropped my chin to my chest, thinking. I had the Druid I would need to block the Necromancer's exit. I had a witch at my back and two shifters that would go with me, regardless of whether or not they were one hundred percent.

But there was still that niggling piece of doubt in the back of my mind, courtesy of O'Shea. If I'd never worked with him, I never would have started to question the 'why' of things. The easy thing to assume was that the Necromancer was a pervert, was using the children's bodies for things I'd rather not think about. But that didn't explain the way the house had been set up, as if the kids were well cared for, even in death.

"Where's Kyle?"

Agent Valley looked over his shoulder. "In the back office, pissing his pants the last time I checked."

Giving Agent Valley a nod, I strode past him, heading to the office I'd first been interrogated in. Excuse me, introduced to the 'team.'

I didn't knock on the door, just walked right in, startling Kyle. He shot out of his seat, his face pale, eyes so wide they looked like he might have been doing drugs if I didn't know better.

"Are the zombies dead?"

"Yes. Are you done crapping your pants?" I leaned against the table and smiled at him. He blanched even more. Good. He had a long way to go before he got back in my good books. "You need to get on your little computer and pull up some files for me."

Kyle nodded rapidly. "Yeah, of course. What do you need?"

"Brittany Mariana Tolvay. She's a kid that died a long time ago. Find out if there are any relatives still living, what happened to her, anything you can. And make it snappy, I don't have all fucking day."

He scrambled to the closest computer and within ten seconds his shaking had subsided. I pulled a chair out, sat down, and leaned my head back so I could stare up at the ceiling and let my mind go blank. For just a moment, I wanted to not think about anything.

It didn't last long.

Kyle pushed his chair back with a screech. "Okay, I've got her. She has one living relative, but I'm thinking it must be a mistake. Same name as her mother, right down to the date of birth. Year is wrong, of course."

I pushed myself to my feet and went over to his computer, staring at the screen.

Kyle continued to talk, his nerves showing in the rapid fire of his words. "Brittany was killed by influenza, so was her father. Mother survived but went missing within weeks of the kid's death." He tapped a few keys and a grainy picture came up of a tall woman, hair pulled back in a severe bun, wearing a long dark dress that covered her from her ankles to her chin. "This is her mother. Anne Tolvay. But this is the part that gets creepy." He tapped a few more keys and a color photo, looked like it was a driver's license shot, came up. The same woman now in living color. Her hair was yanked into the same severe bun and her eyes stared straight ahead, a blankness to them that I recognized all too well. I'd seen it more than once on Giselle's face. Shit, were we dealing with a crazy Necromancer?

I tapped the screen and the computer hissed at me, the monitor going fuzzy. I stepped back. "Where's this picture from?"

Kyle drummed the keys again, fingers flying. "Garden West Home for the Insane."

That's what I was worried about. "Can you pull up her files?"

He didn't say yes or no, just got back to work. I knew from experience it wouldn't take him long.

The door to the office creaked open; Pamela stuck her head in.

"Rylee, I think you'd better come out here."

"What now?" I grumbled, striding to the door.

She smiled and giggled, though it was a tad bit nervous. "There's a Harpy on the roof."

21

The rooftop was solid, at least; it would take Eve's weight. The Harpy was, to say the least, bedraggled. She was soaked through, her feathers having lost their luster in what must have been a knockdown, drag-out flight across the Atlantic to make it here this fast. Alex bounded, the best he could in his injured state, around her.

"Evie, Evie, Evie!"

Pamela stood back by the door, her eyes wide with awe. I'd asked her to wait for me there and she hadn't argued. I couldn't blame her; a Harpy was nothing to take lightly.

"Eve, I told you that you didn't need to come," I said, throwing my hands into the air. "The case will be over in a matter of hours. What the hell were you thinking?" I wasn't doing my best imitation of calm, but I couldn't help it. The last thing I needed was another lost soul to deal with. The case was difficult enough as it was.

She clacked her beak at me, eyes narrowed. "You are my mentor. I should be with you."

I took a breath and held it. I could do this; I could be a mentor.

Right.

"How did you make it here so fast?" I asked, looking her over. She was dehydrated, her legs were paler than usual, and the exhaustion all but rolled off her.

"I flew straight across."

My jaw dropped. "Eve, you could have died!"

"And you could die without my help," she said, her voice dropping. "You are my family now, you and Alex. No clutch will want me; I have no true training. Not even what Eagle has taught me will be enough for me to stand through the Proving Ceremony."

She'd mentioned this ceremony once before, then brushed it off. Apparently, all Harpies had to prove their abilities. Without training from another Harpy, Eve would never survive the ceremony. She was a complete outcast, as was Alex. As was I.

I scrubbed my hand over my face. "Thank you."

Her head snapped up. "Why would you thank me, are you not angry now?"

"I am angry, but . . . you're right. Family comes first."

The corners of her mouth at the edges of her beak lifted, a Harpy's version of a smile. "Good. Now, what can I do to help?"

"Just" —I lifted my hands— "wait here and rest."

Again, her eyes narrowed, and my struggle with staying calm lost out. "Eve. You will wait here and rest until I say so. Don't fuck around with me."

The Harpy bobbed her head once. "Fine."

"Fine." I spun on my heel and strode to the door leading to the stairwell, where Pamela was waiting with it propped open. A soft sniffle from behind stopped me cold. Shit, Eve was crying. Again. Who knew a Harpy could be so damn emotional?

"Eve, I am glad you're here. Just . . ." I glanced over my shoulder to see her hunched down under an awning on the roof, curling her head underneath her right wing.

Alex stood between us, his eyes sorrowful. "Evie sad."

I made a decision, maybe not the best one, but one that would keep her busy and it might even help. "Eve, as soon as you can, make a circuit of the city. We're looking for zombies, disturbed graveyards, and O'Shea."

Her head snapped up. "O'Shea?"

I kept my voice even. "Milly has him. So if you see them, keep your distance."

"I can go right now—"

"No, rest first, and then go."

Giving me one last bob of her head, no more tears followed, thank the gods.

Alex, Pamela, and I headed down the stairwell, the echo of our footsteps bouncing wildly around us.

Kyle met us half way up. "I've got the files you wanted."

Trotting down the rest of the stairs, I slammed open the stairwell door into the main office and jogged to the office. On screen was Anne Tolvay's picture again, her file in black and white.

I read out loud, mostly because I could barely believe what I was seeing.

"Tolvay believes herself the mother of a child dead over a hundred years ago. Insists that she can raise the dead, has tried to kill several nurses just so she can prove that she has the ability to raise them from the dead."

Kyle stepped up beside me. "That's nothing. Check this out."

He moved the mouse and clicked it on the next page.

"Tolvay escapes after claiming she can save children from death; claims she can keep them alive forever."

"Is there anything else?" I asked, my mind reeling with the information.

"Well, there's lots in her files, but do you need more?" Kyle made a move as if to show me another page, but he was right. I didn't really need anything else.

I waved at him to stop. "No, this is enough. But . . ."

Silence thickened between us. The hum of the computer and the ticking of the office clock the only noises in the room.

"But what?"

I thought about the look in Anne's eyes from the pictures. She was mad, of that I was certain. Was it because of her Necromancer abilities? Was it the same kind of curse Giselle had, where the more Anne used her abilities, the more she lost herself to the madness?

A tired sigh slipped out of me. Lately, there had been no open and shut cases. Nothing that was 'just find the kid and take him home'. I felt like someone was out to test me, to push me to my limits and see what would make me break.

Life could be a bitch like that.

"Kyle, round up Deanna, Will, Pamela, Alex, and Agent Valley. I'll brief them and then we're going in."

He ran to do as I asked, my now ever faithful servant, the little rat bastard. Leaning against the wall, I did a mental run-through. I had more than enough weapons, and I had plenty of help, but still, I felt as though it wasn't enough. Like I was missing something.

I closed my eyes and leaned my head back, again feeling fatigue creep up along my vertebrae. Blame it on the jet lag. Or the lack of sleep the night before. Or the fact that there was so much to do once this case was done.

O'Shea.

Berget.

Jack.

Pamela and Alex came into the room, followed by Deanna, Will, Kyle, and Agent Valley.

"Kyle," I said, and he looked up as he sat down. "Get out. This isn't a meeting for you."

He frowned, caught himself, and then gave me a weak smile. "Right. Sorry." He scooted back out the door—his face red—and closed it behind him with a click.

Did I feel bad that I'd embarrassed him? Not for one instant.

"The Necromancer we're dealing with is, for lack of a better term, nuts. She's stealing the children—"

"Wait, she?" Deanna asked.

"Yeah, she. Her daughter died, and now I think she's trying to replace her daughter with the bodies of other children."

Will leaned forward and put his elbows on the table. "How are we going to catch her?"

Thanks the gods he could get straight to the point. "I'll Track the kids, when we get close, Deanna you will block her access to the Veil."

Deanna nodded. "I can do that."

I shrugged. "Then we go in and put her down."

Agent Valley choked. "Put her down?"

I laced my fingers in my lap. "Okay, we go in and kill her. That better?"

His eyes nearly bugged out of his head. "You can't do that."

"You can't keep her in an institution. She's broken out once," I snapped. "Besides, Necromancers live for a long time. Very, very long. As in hundreds of years. How are you going to explain that to the institution, assuming you actually managed to keep her in one?"

The FBI agent was shaking his head. "No, I can't let you do that."

"Then kids are going to continue to be snatched in their final moments, the ones that they should be spending with their families."

Agent Valley continued to shake his head and I knew that it was over. Whatever tenuous relationship the FBI and I had was done. Finito. He was always going to revert to what he knew best: rules. Rules I only knew how to break.

"That is not how we work," he said.

"I thought I had free rein."

"Not like this."

Shrugging, I stepped away from the wall. "Fine. You explain to Interpol that the one person who could

Track this baby-raising bitch down just quit." I strode past him, deliberately butting my shoulder against his, shoving him with my body. Sure, it was immature, but he was pissing me off with his flip-flopping. First I was in charge, then I wasn't. I should never have brought him in on the details. Lesson learned.

Pamela caught up to me first. "You aren't really going to leave those kids with her, are you?"

I shook my head, and called back over my shoulder. "Will, Deanna. You coming?"

Will gave me a wink. "Of course. We wouldn't miss this for the world."

Agent Valley stepped out of the office just before I turned my back on him. "Adamson, don't you dare cross me on this!"

I put a hand over my heart. "Me? Oh, hell no. I'm going to have a nap. No rules against that, is there?"

His eyes narrowed, a sign that he knew I was still going after the Necromancer, regardless of what I was saying. We'd have a tail, at the least.

Of course, I'll admit I was kinda looking forward to them trying to tail a Harpy.

22

Will and Deanna sat on the battered up blue couch in my suite while I spread out my weapons on the floor.

My hand hovered over the crossbow. I hadn't had a lot of time with it, but what I'd been able to see so far was promising. The bolts had been firing straight and clean, hitting the targets when I'd practiced.

I slipped the strap over my shoulder. A little distance between me and the zombies was not a bad thing. The remembrance of my flesh being yanked from my body with teeth was still too fresh to deny the shiver of fear of it happening again. Torn apart by dulled and rotting teeth. Not a pretty thought.

"How are we going to shake them?" Will asked.

Leaning to the left, I could just see out the bottom half of the living room window and the pair of uniforms that were standing at the edge of the walkway.

"Subtle, aren't they?"

Wringing her hands in her lap, Deanna shifted in her seat. "I don't see how this is going to work."

I sat back on my heels. "The kids are to the south now, way south." I concentrated working out the distance in my head. "I'm going to say close to two hundred miles." Deanna's mouth opened, and I talked over her head. "Will, Pamela, and Alex are going to go for a drive. Round about. Lose the tail, and then they'll head south to meet us."

Will cleared his throat. "How will we find you?"

"You won't. I'll find you. Just head south."

Frowning, the Druid stared at me. "And what about us?"

"We're going to go straight there."

"How?"

I smiled. "Eve will take us."

Her face paled. "You mean the Harpy? I don't think that's safe."

"I'm sorry, did you think this was a picnic? Did you think that going after a mad Necromancer was going to be safe?" I laughed at her. "I can see why Daniels is taking over your Coven or whatever the hell a bunch of Druids is called. You're a fucking sissy."

Will looked to me, and then to his sister. "Deanna, you knew what was going to be asked of you."

"You'd side with her?" His sister glared at him.

"You sided with my Destruction against me."

Deanna paled. Ooh, that was a shot to the gut.

I stood up, shouldering the crossbow, and checking all the sheath straps on my body. Everything was secure. Pointedly, I ignored Deanna and her outrage, her fervently whispered words to Will. Did I need the Druid? Yes, 100 percent. But if she was going to question how we were doing things, she wouldn't be a help; she'd just be a serious liability. Not exactly what I wanted, but it wouldn't be the first time someone who was supposed to help me backed out at the last second. Of course, that made me think about Milly, which made me think about the fact that she'd ensnared O'Shea. Which only served to blacken my mood further.

"Are you coming with me or not?" I asked.

Deanna shook her head. "I'll not come with you, no." I glared at her and she held up her hand. "I said I'd help you and I will. I'll go with William."

Not exactly what I was hoping for, but better than a poke in the eye with a fork.

Pamela put her hands on her hips and glared at the Druid. "You know what, I'm glad you aren't going. You just showed me what you Druids are really like. Even if you tried to take me to your stupid Druids, I wouldn't go. You're a coward."

My eyebrows shot into my hairline. The witch was a spitfire, I'd give her that.

With a flounce in her step, she moved to my side. "I'll come with you."

I put a hand on her shoulder. "Okay, let's go. Will?" His eyes met mine and I held his gaze. "Make it snappy."

"You got it."

Alex whimpered. "Alex wants to go with Rylee and Evie and Pamie." His tail thumped weakly on the floor and he put his front paws together, begging. "Please."

I crouched down, lifted up one of his floppy ears, and did a stage whisper into it, making sure Will heard me. "You need to keep an eye on the kitty and the Druid for me. Okay? Make sure they don't do anything wrong."

Before I let go of his ear, he was nodding, and then he wrinkled his lips up over his teeth in a ridiculous grin that made my heart squeeze. Gods, what would I do without Alex? What a horrible, boring, stale life I would lead.

Pamela and I headed out first to the police station. For once, the seemingly incessant rain had eased. Perfect for flying in. Well, maybe not perfect, but better than being pelted with fat rain hundreds of feet in the air.

We nodded at the two officers who stepped in behind to follow us; I felt their footsteps stutter when Will, Deanna, and Alex came out of the suite and headed toward the car.

Decisions, decisions.

I draped an arm across Pamela's shoulders. "When we get to the police station, your job is to pin anyone who tries to stop us to the wall. Just hold them there. Can you do that?"

She smiled. "Yes. And now I can tie off the spell so I don't have to be in the room to hold them."

This kid was way beyond what I expected in talent. Giselle and her predictions; who knew that even in her madness she was trying to help?

"When did you have time to practice?"

"When I was sitting in the tree. I started pinning the bugs up so they wouldn't crawl on me."

Laughing, we walked into the police station. The looks we got from the officers ranged from outright disgust—I suppose a child hacking off zombie limbs would do that—to fear, to curiosity, right down to anger.

Of course, the anger was coming from one Dr. Daniels limping toward us. "There she is! She attacked me and sent me to the hospital with a sword wound! I have the hospital paperwork to prove it. I am taking the child away from her right—"

Dr. Daniels was picked up and slammed against the far wall. Pamela glowered at her. "I'm staying with Rylee."

Then, of course, everything sort of hit the fan. Officers rushed to help the doctor; officers rushed us. Pamela did an admirable job pinning up people. Like flies on sticky tape they hung anywhere from three feet to seven feet up the wall. Some she hung upside down, sideways, and diagonal.

Agent Valley came out of the main office, spluttering with rage. But it was the twinkle in his eyes and the quirk to his lips that told me I'd once again been played. I figured it out in the heartbeat before Pamela picked him up and pinned him to the ceiling.

He wanted me to do this, wanted me to break the rules. That way it wasn't on the FBI's shoulders if it went wrong.

The greasy little manipulator!

Well, we'd just see how smart everyone thought he was.

"Agent Valley, thank you for clearing the path for us. As always, it's a pleasure doing business with the FBI. But next time, my fees will be double."

His whole body spasmed against the ceiling and when he opened his mouth, Pamela gagged him.

"How did you know?" I asked as we sauntered through the building to the stairwell leading up to the roof.

"I thought he was going to say something mean to you again. And I didn't want him to."

Her words were an eerie echo of Alex. The two of them both wanted to protect me, and all I wanted was to make sure they were safe. A dark premonition trickled along my senses, making my gut twist. There would come a day when their loyalty would get them killed. Before that happened, I would have to send them on their way.

We ran up the stairs, but I was lost in my thoughts. I knew why Jack was alone. There was so much danger involved with being a Tracker. And for some stupid reason we inspired loyalty in those we were supposed to be protecting.

Bursting out the top door onto the roof, I heard shouting below.

"The spell must have worn off." Pamela frowned. "I'm sorry, I thought it would last longer."

"Don't worry about it." I looked around for something to jam the door with. Eve could be tricky to wake up and if her head jammed under her wing was any indication, she was deep in sleep. Which meant I needed a little more time. The roof was littered with garbage pipe, leftovers from some renovation or another. I grabbed the closest piece that was about four feet long and jammed it under the door handle, burying the end in the loose gravel of the roof.

"Eve," I shouted from where I was. "I need you to wake up. We've got problems!"

The Harpy grumbled in her sleep and lifted her head. "Rylee?"

"Yeah, we've got—"

The door thumped from the other side, the weight of a few officers behind it.

"You awake enough to take me and Pamela for a fly about?"

Eve ruffled her wings. She'd only gotten a few hours sleep and I knew I was asking a lot of her. Now I was glad she'd come, though I had been less than grateful when she'd first landed.

With a beak-clacking yawn, she nodded. "Yes, I can take you two."

I pushed Pamela ahead of me and we ran to Eve's side. We skidded to a stop and I was in the middle of boosting Pamela up when the door banged open. Agent Valley was at the front of the pack.

"ADAMSON!"

I gave him a wave, and then blew him a kiss. "You got it, boss. I'm on the case, just like you said!"

Leaping up behind Pamela, I wrapped my arms around her and buried my hands in Eve's feathers. The Harpy launched straight up, her powerful wings sweeping out around us in a gust of wind and dust. When I looked down, the rooftop crawled with people. Denning had finally shown up, though he'd been MIA since before the zombie attack. By the looks of things as we banked to the south, Denning and Valley were arguing. At least, Valley took a swing at Denning just before we lost them from sight.

"Just head south, Eve. And stay high enough that we can't be seen from the ground."

"Not a problem," she said.

Pamela shivered and I tightened my arms around her. Though in some ways she reminded me of Berget, in others she was completely opposite. Her coloring, of course, her age was close to what Berget would be now, and her loyalty. But Berget had never had a feisty bone in her; in that, Pamela was so different. I had to believe that whoever had taken Berget had treated her well, because I doubted she would have survived otherwise. Pamela, on the other hand, would survive with or without me. She was, in some ways, more like me than I'd thought at first.

Already, she was growing and changing, her acceptance of this new world she'd been introduced to as natural as if she'd been born to it. A blessing and curse all rolled into a tidy little package, one that she would have her entire life, however long that would end up being.

I Tracked the kids and sat bolt upright. Fuck, the Necromancer had moved them! I felt the pull as strongly as before, a tether that circled around and pulled me in the opposite direction of where we were headed.

"Eve, swing around. The kids have been moved."

Pamela sucked in a breath. "How will Alex and Deanna and Will find us?"

I grit my teeth as Eve banked hard to the left, her body slicing through the skim of clouds around us.

"They won't."

23

Milly had him standing with his nose pressed into the corner of her hotel room, like he was some ill-behaved child. He could hear and smell, but that was it. The witch's perfume was overwhelming, the scent of roses so heavy it felt like he was suffocating in it.

The vampire was back, which was what had precipitated O'Shea's current position.

"I'm telling you, I have complete control over him," Milly snapped.

"Witch. I wasn't asking." There was the sound of a slap, and while O'Shea wasn't overly fond of the vampire, he wished he could have seen Milly get smacked around.

"You bastard, I'll make you pay for that," she screeched. "Liam, kill him!"

He spun and leapt at the vampire, toppling him to the ground. For once, he agreed with the command Milly gave him, and it made all the difference. His body unleashed all the pent up frustration and need to kill, and teeth and claws ripped through flesh as he pummeled the vampire with everything he had. That lasted all of twenty seconds before Faris put an end to it.

Faris laughed, his hands shooting out toward Liam, clamping the agent's arms flat to his sides, effectively stopping O'Shea from moving. As if he were a child.

"Oh, wolf, if only you knew the power you carried, you'd be a formidable opponent. One worthy of my time and efforts." The vampire shifted his head to one side. "As it is, you are a royal pain in my ass— and until Rylee realizes you aren't coming back, I think it's safe to say you are very much in my way."

With a quick flick, Faris removed the torc while Milly screamed.

O'Shea scrambled back from him, his hands going involuntarily to his throat. "Why would you help me?"

Laughing, Faris smiled down at him. "Is that what you think I did?"

Before he could say anything else, O'Shea felt it, the pressure that had been unleashed. Milly had made sure the wolf was buried—the wolf and whatever else lay inside of him.

With a pained howl, he grabbed his head, the force of the wolf building until his skin split and the beast roared forward, all sense of humanity fleeing.

Faris continued his lecture. "You see, wolf, when you stop the natural progression of something, particularly in our world, it builds. Like an avalanche growing as it scours a mountainside. And if you unleash it after all that time building." He made a popping sound with his tongue on the roof of his mouth.

The witch lifted her hand and Faris was suddenly on her, his face inches from hers. "If you want my continued protection, Milly, I suggest you re-think your next action."

Sniffling, she managed to speak. "It's been too long, the torc shouldn't have come off."

The vampire continued to smile. "I know."

"Why don't you just kill him then?"

Faris tsked. "The only reason I don't kill him now is that I want Rylee to trust me. She can't do that if I kill the man she loves, can she?"

He turned his face back to Liam. "Happy hunting, wolf. Just so you know, there will be no coming back for you."

O'Shea's entire world crumbled as the wolf took full control, wiping out his humanity in one fell swoop. Though he tried to hang on, O'Shea and everything he was got pushed back, deep into the recesses of his mind.

His last human thought was of her. The girl with the tri-colored eyes, the girl whose name had already fled, but the scent and image, the touch and feel of her was burned into his soul so deep that even the wolf couldn't extinguish her. She was his mate, forever, his all, his heart.

Hope flickered.

She would come for him.

It felt like a nasty case of déjà vu with a slight twist.

Pamela and I were crouched on the rooftop of an older four-story home in the countryside, the Necromancer below us inside the confines of the home. Now that I knew who she was and had seen her picture, I could Track her as well as the kids. Her mind was a jumble of emotions fighting to be heard, clamoring overtop of one another. I blocked her and focused on the kids.

"What now?" Pamela asked, her hand gripping the handle of the long knife I'd given her. I pulled my crossbow off my back and set a bolt in the channel.

"We go in quietly, see if we can't knock her out and get the opal on her. It'll be the only way without Deanna here to help."

Pamela nodded. "And there'll be zombies, won't there?"

"Yes. But they're slow. Let me go first, I'll clear the way. You finish off any that I wound. Okay? But no magic unless you absolutely have to."

"All right."

Eve had already headed south, though she'd argued with me about it. Finally, though, she'd agreed when I'd pointed out that Alex, Will, and Deanna had no idea where we were, and there was no way we had to contact them.

Setting the butt of the crossbow tight into my shoulder, I crept forward. The rooftop was mainly an open solarium, half-dead plants wilting in their pots, tile set into the roof for footing, and even a few garden statues.

We moved quickly, looking for the way down into the house. Pamela found it after a few minutes of looking, partially buried under a large pot filled with dirt and a withered stick that maybe at one point had been a tree or bush.

"Here, we'll lift it together," I said, gripping the edge of the old copper flowerpot.

With a heave, we rolled it sideways with almost no sound. So far so good.

I crouched and slid one hand over the rusted latch. Jaw tight, I pulled it as slowly as I could, praying for a silent mechanism. There was a muffled screech of metal on rusted metal. Wincing, I gave up the subtlety, wrenched the latch open, and jerked the trap door upward.

It gave way, the hinges mercifully silent, though I wasn't sure how much that would help us now. I peered down into the blackness of what appeared to be the attic. Maybe no one had heard the noise? I Tracked the kids; they were all still here, only a floor or two below us.

"Leave the door open and wait for me to give you the okay," I said, swinging the crossbow onto my back and then lowering myself through the trapdoor.

Dropping to the floor below, I waited in a perfectly-still crouch. The darkness seemed benign for once.

"Pamela."

"Coming," she whispered, lowering herself to hang from the lip of the trap door and then dropping to land beside me.

"Light," I said, keeping my voice low.

She lifted her hand and a soft pink glow lit up around her fingers.

"Perfect," I said, getting a good look at the room. Indeed, this was an attic. Across from us was an old steamer trunk, its lid flung open, contents pouring out of it like someone had been looking for something. I looked inside of it, the smell of age whispering up around me.

A name was etched into the underside of the lid. Brittany Mariana Tolvay. This was the daughter's trunk. I bent and picked up a skirt, far too small for an adult. These were her things.

An idea began to form as I thought about what had brought Anne Tolvay to this point. Giselle had been mad at the end, totally and completely mad. But did that make her a bad person? Was it her fault that the madness had taken over and made her do things that she otherwise never would have?

"Pamela, I think we can end this without anyone getting hurt."

Her blue eyes flicked up to mine, far too perceptive for her age. "You want me to wear her clothes, don't you?"

I pawed through the trunk, finding a drab black dress. "You wearing her clothes will do two things. It'll be a distraction for the Necromancer, and it'll help to keep you safe. If she thinks you are her long dead daughter . . . " Bunching up the starchy material, I pulled it down over Pamela's head as I finished my thought. ". . .you will be able to get close to her. Or at least, she won't fuck off using the Veil as a jump point. If it looks like she's going to make a run for it, call out to her."

Pamela wiggled, straightening the dress out. The black old school dress was the right length but it was loose around the slight girl. "What should I say?"

I thought for a moment. "Mother or mama. With you here, if she believes you're her daughter, I don't think she'll jump the veil. Are you ready?"

"Yup, I got it."

As ready as we could be, I led the way to the door leading out of the attic. Cracking it open a sliver, I could just see the narrow stairwell leading down to the next floor.

"Stay behind me," I said. Crossbow up and ready to fire, I crept slowly down the stairs.

The air around us seemed to tense the further down we went, or perhaps it was just my nerves. This Anne Tolvay had fucked off on me once; I couldn't let it happen again. My gut was telling me it was now or never.

On the first landing we came to, there was only one zombie. I pulled the trigger on the crossbow and the mechanism fired with a soft twang, the bolt taking the zombie between the eyes and pinning it to the wall. It convulsed once and then sagged, what was left of its life leaking out of it and down the paisley wallpaper.

A quick check of the rooms on that level showed nothing. I Tracked the kids; they were still here, all bunched together. Dread slid through my heart, the sick knowledge that we were about to see twenty-plus kids in a state of half decay and worse. Fuck. I tried to shake it off, but the feeling clung to me.

The next stairwell down was empty, and then we were on the landing of the second floor. The kids were across the landing behind the second door on the left.

Of course, that's when that bitch of a Necromancer sprung her little trap.

And we'd walked right the fuck into it.

24

Zombies poured out from the other three doors, climbed the stairs from below us, and forced us back the way we'd come.

I shot three in the head in quick succession, but it was too tight of quarters for the crossbow to be as effective as it could be. Booting the closest zombie in the chest, I slung my crossbow over my shoulder and pulled my two swords.

"Stay on the stairs," I yelled, catching Pamela out the corner of my eye doing as I told her. At least she listened.

Then it was all limbs and bodies being hacked, and I wondered if the flood of rotters would ever end. There were too many for me to take on, more even than had been at the police station.

"Rylee, let me help," Pamela said, the terror in her voice obvious.

"Not yet," I grunted.

Three more decapitations and I'd made a little room around me, though with the pile up of bodies, it wasn't much.

Time to bring out the big guns.

"Anne Tolvay," I shouted as I spun, taking the arm off a zombie reaching past me to Pamela. "I have your daughter, Brittany!"

An unearthly howl rent the air and the zombies shuffled to a stop, their mouths hanging open, eyes vacant.

"Quick, Pamela. Get behind me so she can only see the dress. Keep your face hidden."

Pamela leapt toward me, grabbing my belt for balance. I jabbed one sword into the body of the nearest zombie so I could reach back and hang onto Pamela. Just in case.

The door opened and Anne Tolvay stepped out, her cheeks streaked with tears. Her bun was in complete disarray, and her clothing looked like she'd been wearing it for weeks, maybe longer.

She leaned to see around me, gasping at the glimpse of her daughter's dress. Her hands flew to her mouth. "My precious Brittany," she sobbed. "Come, come to mama." She had a heavy Russian accent, but her English was perfect. I might as well have not been there, as she reached out to Pamela.

"Anne," I said, keeping my voice low. She didn't respond. "Anne!"

Her eyes jerked to mine. "Who are you? And why do you keep me from my child?"

The zombies came back to life and started toward us. "They will kill Brittany," I said, slashing, taking a zombie off at the waist, viscera spilling out and causing other zombies to topple like a macabre game of dominos.

"They will never harm my daughter."

Shit, this was not going as I planned. I had to get her to stop.

"Then I'll kill her myself!"

Anne screeched and Pamela clung to me. I gave her a squeeze and she relaxed.

"Do not harm my daughter, please. I've been looking for her. I will reward you greatly if you give her back to me."

The madness had completely taken Anne's mind, and if I hadn't experienced the loss of Giselle's own lucidity, I might not have felt as I did. As it was, I didn't want to hurt Anne, even though she'd hurt so many people.

"Send the zombies away. Then we can talk."

Anne clapped her hands and shouted something in Russian, and the zombies shuffled down the steps one at a time like perfect soldiers. The thought that she, Anne, could unleash the undead on a city gave me a shiver. There was no way the humans would survive if that ever happened; it would be just like all their movies depicting the end of the world, one full of rotters.

Anne stood across from me, worry lines etched in her forehead. "Please, I just want to see her, to make sure she's okay."

Oh boy, time to throw the dice. Very slowly I pulled Pamela out beside me as I whispered, "Keep your head down and if you have to talk, keep it short and sweet."

Pamela gave the slightest tremor of her head acknowledging me, and then I lifted my eyes to see the Necromancer's reaction.

Her hands were palms together in front of her lips. "My sweet babushka." She lowered her hands and her faded blue eyes lifted to mine. "What do you want of me?"

"You have other children here."

She nodded, lowered her eyes. "I could not bear to be alone. But they . . . they didn't need their families anymore. Death stalked them. I gave them life." Her voice grew in intensity as she spouted her beliefs.

Shifting my weight to my heels, I tensed, expecting an attack. "It's time for them to go back to their families."

Nodding, her hair floated out around her face. "Yes, now that Brittany is here." She smiled, her lips trembling as she reached for Pamela, who I could see was fighting her natural inclination to shrink away from the crazy woman in front of us.

"You and I are going to take those kids back to the hospital," I said. "Brittany." I squeezed Pamela's shoulder. "Will wait here for us."

Anne put her hands over her heart. "Of course, of course. What you say, it makes perfect sense. These babies don't need me."

She turned her back and stepped into the room she'd come from.

I spoke quickly. "Just wait here, go up to the roof and hide."

"You think she'll try to come back without you?"

"Yes, I'm almost sure of it."

"What if she—"

"If she takes you, I can find you no matter where you go. I won't leave you with her if it comes to that." I touched the side of her face. "Trust me."

Pamela nodded, and I left her standing there in a dead girl's dress, trusting that I wouldn't let her down.

As I crossed through the open door, I couldn't stop myself from recoiling, almost falling backwards.

What lay on the floor and in the cribs spread about the room was worse than any adult zombie I'd seen. Little limbs, little teeth, ears half-falling off, flesh peeling away from miniature rib cages, the stench of death and rotting flesh. A hint of baby powder and lilacs, as if someone had tried to cover the smell. Fingers reaching toward me, eyes missing and glazed over, clumps of hair caught in teeth and fingers. I gagged, biting my tongue to keep the puke in, bile coating my throat. This was the stuff of nightmares.

"Come along, babies, time to go!" Anne called cheerfully—as if this was normal, which for her it was, of course, but FUCK—and the babies did just as the adult zombies did. They lined up and toddled, crawled, walked, and wormed their way to Anne. She made a slash with her hand and the air parted in front of her. I could see the hospital furnace room, the first place I'd Tracked her to.

"Holy fuck," I whispered. She could *make* entryways into the Veil. That's how she'd been jumping around so easily!

Anne gave me a dirty look. "Please, no bad language in front of the children. Hurry babies, time to go." She directed them and they crossed the Veil easily, disappearing one by one.

I drew closer, seeing the children spread out on the floor. "You have to release them."

Anne drew herself up, breathing in deep. "I love them all so much. You don't have a child; I can see it in you. You can't possibly understand the grief of losing a child so young."

I hated that I felt compassion for her, that my heart understood all too well. "I think you'd be surprised by what I know."

She turned to face me, denim blue eyes piercing into mine as if she searched me for the truth. "Perhaps you are right."

A flick of her hand and the babies stiffened as a unit, slowly slumping to the concrete floor. "Sleep well, my sweet darlings. Your love carried me through so many years."

Creepy as hell? Yes. But again, I saw too much of Giselle in Anne, the same kind of madness that made them say and do things that were so—

She shoved me, catching the edge of my shoulder as she tried to force me to cross the Veil.

"And I felt sorry for your half-rotted ass," I said as I used her momentum, grabbed her arm, and pulled her with me, through the Veil and into the furnace room. She screeched and reached back the way we'd come, the threshold still open. Pamela ran to peer in.

"Go," I yelled as I wrestled with Anne. She had almost no muscle strength I could feel and so it wasn't much of a contest, but when she raised her hand and the babies twitched I knew I had to get the hell out of there. Like now.

A swift twist of my arm and I was free of Anne's grip. Leaping through the Veil back to the house, I crashed onto the floor on the other side and spun on my knees, sword raised. The slash in the air was gone. The thump of feet going up the stairs told me Pamela was on the move.

The stomps coming up the stairs told me Anne was pissed. Of course, the bottleneck of the lower stairway worked to my advantage. Stepping up, I starting removing heads as they came into range. One after another, the zombies kept lurching and struggling forward over their dead comrades.

After only a few minutes, I stepped back. I didn't like leaving Pamela on her own, even if she was a powerful witch in her own right.

Leaping and lunging up the stairs to the third floor, I kept a sharp ear for the zombies below me. Upside? They were slow, no fleet-footed runners in the bunch. Downside? They were still coming and wouldn't stop until they'd been killed or Anne turned them off— which I was betting wouldn't be anytime soon.

I hit the trapdoor with my shoulder, shoving it open onto the roof, climbing up and through.

Anne had beat me there.

Scrambling, I spun out on the tiles as I slammed the trapdoor shut, my eyes never leaving the scene in front of me. Pamela was backed against the far edge of the roof, and Anne was advancing on her, crooning in Russian.

I lifted the crossbow without a thought. Feeling sorry for Anne didn't mean I'd let her hurt, or take, Pamela.

The bolt fired seamlessly and slammed into Anne's spine, right between her shoulder blades. She screeched and spun, her hands curling into hooked claws they twisted so much.

"You would keep me from my child?"

"She's not yours to take," I said. This had gone far enough. The kids were returned home and as much as I didn't want to kill Anne, it had to be done.

"Your mentor would be disappointed in you. Her spirit hovers close, disapproving." Anne said and the grip on my crossbow faltered.

"She is not here." My voice, though, was not steady. Fuck, was Giselle really here? If anyone would know, it would be a Necromancer.

Anne shook her head. "You have lost more than I realized. I see the bodies around you now, the death that clings to your shoulders. Those who love you, they die. But you live. I know this pain better than any other."

I shook, hard—hard enough that I knew I'd never get a good shot off. Dropping the crossbow, I pulled a sword from its sheath. "Life's a bitch." I took three running steps. "And then you die." Before I could slam my sword home, she was yanked into the air away from me, her arms pinned to her sides, a surprised look etched into her face.

Pamela stood across from me. "I don't think you should kill her. She isn't really bad. Is she? We can put the amulet on her now."

I closed my eyes, feeling the weight of what I'd almost done and why. I'd been ready to kill Anne to shut her up, to keep her from saying the things I already knew and avoided thinking about at all costs. And in the past it would have been fine, but with Pamela watching, well, I was going to have to curb my innate tendency to kill first and ask later. Maybe I was going to have to learn to do some growing up of my own.

"No, she isn't really bad. Just sick." I lowered the sword and gave Pamela a tired, worn the fuck out smile. "You did the right thing."

The young witch smiled at me, her face lighting up. She lowered Anne back to the roof.

Anne smiled down on her, a sense of contentment and happiness rolling off her entire frame. "My sweet babushka, saving Mother."

My fingers went to my pocket and the stone there, the stone that would give Anne lucidity. The stone Giselle had said I would need, and I'd almost ignored. I pulled it out, then without asking, slipped it over her head.

25

As it turned out, Will, Deanna, and Alex were a long time in showing up. But with Anne back in full control of her faculties, she put the zombies down. To be safe, though, we waited on the roof. Just in case.

Pamela and I sat playing twenty questions and "I Spy" to pass the time. Now that she was lucid, Anne even joined in. Yes, it was weird to be playing childish games with a woman that only a short time before had tried to kill me via her zombies. Then again, she seemed almost normal. The crossbow bolt had done very little damage. What I didn't know when I shot her was that Necromancers could pull energy from the dead to heal. Anne explained it all to us while we waited, like we were in some sort of supernatural convention.

"The dead have energy, just as the living do," Anne said, her head tipped to one side. "It is how we live so long. It is why I could keep the madness at bay as long as I did."

I lifted my foot and put my boot on the edge of the roof wall. "Brittany was burned, that's why you couldn't raise her, isn't it?"

Anne gave me a sad smile. "Yes, it was the practice then to burn the bodies, cleansing them so the sickness wouldn't pass. The madness came on after that, slowly, but still . . . "

Pamela wrinkled her nose and slipped out of the long black dress. Anne's eyes still tracked Pamela's movements, though she clearly knew it wasn't her daughter. The Necromancer's eyes were full of longing for something she couldn't have.

Will and Alex were the first to reach us. Actually, Alex was the first one.

I stood at the sound of the trapdoor lifting and then a bolt of black fur and long tongue rushed me, bowling me over and licking my face. "Rylee, Rylee, Rylee, Rylee, Rylee." Actually it came out like "Lylee," but I suppose that was the best he could do while licking.

"Good to see you too, buddy," I said, pushing him off me, not unkindly. He continued to bounce around, then came to a stuttering stop when he got close to Anne.

"She's a stinky one." He pinched the tip of his nose with two claws.

Deanna climbed up through the trapdoor and I peeked down. "What happened to all the zombies?" She glanced down. "They're just laying there, dead."

I lifted an eyebrow. "They were dead before."

She put one hand on her hip. "You know what I mean. I'm no expert on the dead, it isn't my specialty. Why aren't they all doing their zombie-shuffle thing?"

Anne spoke up. "I have released them all."

I heard the ring of truth in her words. "What now? How are we going to finish this? The stone will only keep the madness at bay for a little while. It isn't a cure."

The Necromancer stared at me. "I have lost, I am done. You know what I am; will you let me live? Of course not. The child saved me, but for a moment. My death is inevitable; it is the way of our world. Kill, be killed, or raise the dead. I cannot raise the dead, and killing was never something I enjoyed."

"That only leaves your death," Pamela whispered, yet her words carried to all of us.

Anne gave her gentle smile. "Do not be sad, little one. You will see that it is our way. The Tracker will teach you. I see it in her. She is not like the other Trackers I have known. She has a heart that beats to save, to heal, to bring souls home. It is time for my soul to go home now."

I closed my eyes, my grief for Giselle slipping over my heart, stifling my ability to think. Giselle and Anne, they were two of a kind, their powers stealing their minds. "Is this what you truly want?" I felt the weight of this responsibility fall on me, and truly, who would I give it to? Not Pamela, not Will or Deanna. There was only me.

Anne let out a soft breath. "Let me be with my child in truth. My heart is done with this world."

Gods, this was not supposed to happen, not this way. Her easy acceptance of her death, her wish for it, echoed Giselle's final request. To die the way she wanted to.

I walked over to Anne, only a couple of feet away, perfect striking distance. Never had the sword felt so heavy in my hand.

"Pamela, go stand by Will."

Pamela gave me startled eyes. "But—"

"This is the price some of us pay. Anne has made her choice. I will honor it," I said.

Anne touched her fingers to her lips as Pamela released her. "Your mentor is proud of you. I feel it in the air around us."

I didn't try to stop the sudden onslaught of tears, the loss so keen I felt it to my bones. "Tell her—"

"I will."

There were no more words, just the slice of my blade through the air, the pause of life as Anne closed her eyes one last time, the thump of her headless body as it slumped to the roof . . . and the tinkle of the opal as it rolled to my feet.

I bent, scooped the opal up, and wiped a smear of blood off the chain before slipping it into my pocket.

26

The kids Anne had under her thrall were still in the boiler room when we led the SOCA team there. I Tracked little Sophia, her blanket in my hands. She was in the far corner, her body barely recognizable as human, never mind a child's. I spread the blanket over her, giving her a final goodbye of my own. None of the parents were allowed to see the bodies, thank the gods for that, and I didn't have to speak to any of them myself—at least, none except for little Johnny's parents. They ran into me in the hallway of the hospital, and I told them he'd been found. But not alive.

They were still grateful, and it ate at me, my heart and soul wishing I could do more. For a brief moment, I understood Anne, the desire to bring back to life that which had been taken from you.

Eve was pleased that we were staying. I wished we could go home, but there were too many loose ends, too many people I loved in trouble here.

There would be no closure for me in London, at least not yet. O'Shea was still missing and I'd be damned if I left him out there stuck with Milly. Which brought me to that particular reality. Milly had to be dealt with. Will agreed to help with her, even going so far as to take a leave from SOCA. He figured it would give him the break he needed both from his job and his Destruction, who apparently were pissed as cats being baptized in a toilet for what had gone on with Daniels and Deanna. Enemies and friends, I seemed to make them without even trying.

Alex healed over the next twenty-four hours, and we got moved to a different basement suite, this one all in yellows that made me want to gouge my eyes out. I tolerated it because it had an extra room for Pamela, who for the moment, I had temporary custody of, much to Dr. Daniels's fury. Agent Valley had come through, finding Pamela's family and getting them to sign her guardianship over to me. Of course, the paperwork had to be finalized in the courts, but pretty much, she was mine.

Pamela was freaking ecstatic.

Finally, I was able to go back to see Jack, my fingers crossed that he was still alive. Pamela was with me this time, as was Alex, of course. Will came along, but only to stand at the door to make sure we weren't bothered.

I didn't bother to knock, and wished to fucking hell I had when I saw Jack and what looked like a pleasantly plump nurse going at it in his bed.

"Damn it, Jack, I've got a kid with me!" I spun and jerked Pamela around so she couldn't see. "You knew I was coming!"

Jack let out a barking laugh. "Don't begrudge me a fuck or two, certainly not with this beauty." At the slap of a hand on bare skin the nurse giggled and a few moments later she passed us in the hall, a decidedly high color on her cheeks.

Shaking my head, I dared a look over my shoulder. Jack was under the covers, by himself this time, a grin from ear to ear.

"Get the fuck in here, girl. Tell me what the bloody fucking hell happened!"

Between Pamela and me, we spun the story out for him, with only the occasional grunt from him added in here and there.

"So, the vamp tried to fuck with your mind, did he?"

"Yeah, you could say that."

"Don't ever let your guard down around that nasty shit. Ever."

I smiled, then frowned at the remembered pleasure Faris had stirred in me. "Yeah, I got that too."

We sat there for a moment, and it was Alex who broke the almost silence.

"Rotters taste like shit."

Jack burst out in a coughing laugh. "They do? Remind me never to fucking eat one."

"Yuppy doody, okee dokee." Alex gave the old Tracker a thumbs up with one hooked claw.

Jack squinted his eyes at me. "You didn't go after your sister yet."

I chewed at the inside of my lip a moment before answering. "She's happy. Healthy. There's nothing wrong with her. I can't give her anything she doesn't already have in spades."

"You think you can just let her go?"

That was the crux of it. I was afraid that I wasn't good enough, that I couldn't give her a better life than

I could already feel her having. There was never a question of whether or not I would find her. I would find her now, that was a given. But I wasn't ready yet to see her, see her happy with another family, and then walk away. Because the reality was, if I brought Berget into my life, she would be in constant danger. Just like Pamela. Except Berget had no ability to protect herself . . . so for now, I was chickening out. If going after a crazy-ass witch and Alpha werewolf who was enthralled by said witch was chickening out.

"No, but I have to find O'Shea first. He's in trouble. Berget . . . if things change, I'll go after her in a heartbeat. But right now . . ." I looked at Jack, stared into his swirling tri-colored blue eyes. "Right now, I need someone to train me before he dies. Can you manage?"

Jack snorted, and patted the sheets down around him. Laughing, his eyes twinkled up at me, the swirl of colors a reminder of what I was, what I would always be. A Tracker to the bitter damn end.

Jack gave me a wink. "You think you're ready to learn what you can really do?"

I laughed, and touched Alex on the head. "What do you think, Alex? You think we should hang out with Jack for a while?

Rippling his lips up over his teeth, Alex started nodding his head at a speed that would have given me whiplash. "Yuppy doody!"

Smiling, I nodded slowly. "I couldn't have said it better myself."

SHADOWED THREADS

A Rylee Adamson Novel
Book 4

"My name is Rylee and I am a Tracker."

When children go missing, and the Humans have no leads, I'm the one they call. I am their last hope in bringing home the lost ones. I salvage what they cannot.

O'Shea is AWOL, and tracking him is proving to be harder than I expected.

Not to mention the small fact that I have the Beast of Bodmin Moor chasing me across Europe in a race against the odds and my life as the prize.

But those things are minor compared to the secrets that finally come to light.

Secrets I wish had stayed hidden in the darkness . . .

$7.99 mass market paperback
978-1-940456-98-0

AN EXCERPT FROM *SHADOWED THREADS*

With my sword, I felt better. Like I could face anything down. I didn't bother to shut the door behind me, just strode back into the hallway. The library was at the far end of the house. Our steps were muffled by the thick rug, which hadn't seen a proper cleaning in what looked like a decade. Pamela struggled to keep up with me without jogging every few steps.

"Jack will be angry. Doesn't that bother you?"

"Jack is going to be angry at me no matter what I do. There comes a time when you can't dick around anymore. And I'm at that moment." I paused in front of the doorway. "This might give me a clue at least as to what the hell is going on, and if he will ever teach me."

"You think it's something bad?" She whispered, her eyes going wide, a glimmer of the child she still was showing through.

Damn, that was exactly what I thought. When he'd promised to teach me, I thought it would take a day or two. Not three weeks of him dodging me.

Which could only mean one thing.

That whatever the hell was going on was no good. Son of a bitch, what was it with the men around me lately that they couldn't just spit things out? Nothing like O'Shea, who always spoke what was on his mind.

Again, a sharp stab of longing gutted me. I breathed in slowly through my nose, working around the pain. Focusing on my task, I lifted my sword and slid it between the two massive doors. Whoever had built the house had done a sloppy job on them. While they did lock, there was a half-inch gap between them. Though it was a tight fit, I could still draw the blade down, slicing through the old lock with very little effort.

"The trick is to make it look like you were never here." I pushed the door open. "Unlike this B&E, where Jack will know that I was here the second he goes to open his door."

She bobbed her head, taking my words in like a sponge. Scary. "You did it that way on purpose then? You want him to know you were in his library?"

I glanced around the library, took it in with a single sweep of my eyes. Two sets of floor-to-ceiling windows that were bordered by long red curtains, also floor to ceiling. Rows and rows of books, again, floor to ceiling. A huge oak table with a few wooden chairs, a couple of overstuffed recliners, and not much else.

"Yes. I want him to know I've had enough of his games." So I would play my own and do my best to force his hand. Either he would teach me, or we would leave. But no more of this shit he was pulling.

Rolling my sword in my hand, it caught the light from a lamp on the big table. I strode to the open book under the light. Open wide, the book was easily three feet across, the words within it written by hand in a scrawling black ink.

I jammed the tip of my sword into the floor at my feet. It would leave a gouge mark on the old wooden slats, but at least it was within easy reach if I needed it. Not that I should, but one can never be too damn careful.

I wrinkled my nose, the musty smell of the pages strong now that I was this close. I grabbed the edge of the book and partially closed it so I could see the front cover. Black leather, a texture that felt familiar to me, but that I couldn't quite place, engraved with a single word.

Demons.

Oh shit, that was just fucking awesome. I grit my teeth and opened the book again, reading the page that Jack had been studying. Had he been trying to find a way to conjure a demon? Maybe to cure him of his cancer? I didn't know if that was even possible, but then again, I didn't really know that much about demons.

"What does it say?" Pamela leaned closer and I pushed her back, not wanting her too close to a book about demons. The one thing I'd learned from Deanna since I'd been here was that witches were susceptible to demons, more than any other super-natural creature. The last thing I wanted was Pamela getting mixed into that shit.

And what about Milly? Yeah, there was a growing suspicion in me that whatever she was up to had to do with more than just a simple vampire . . .

Leaning over the black book, I read it out loud for Pamela.

"And when the Veils shall fall to Orion, there will be no hope for mankind. For with his Rise, the Tracker will die and our glory shall be forever as we bathe in blood and crush those who defy us." I swallowed hard. Shit, that did not sound good. And that name, Orion, it sent fear tracing along my synapses, like my brain wanted me to remember something . . . I couldn't place it though, no matter how many times I read the name. The rest of the page was similar. Orion, whoever the hell he was, would rise, and with him humanity was doomed. We were all doomed by the nasty fucker of a demon. This was not good . . . but why was Jack studying it? Did he think he was the Tracker meant to die?

That would make sense, would explain how freaking cranky he was being.

Pamela moved around the table. "There are more books, made kind of like that one."

She was right, though they were closed and spread out; they were all made with the same kind of leather as the book under my fingers.

I stared at the one furthest from me. The book at the far end was a shade of blue I'd only ever seen on one other supernatural creature.

Dox.

"Shit, these are ogre-skinned books." I stared at them, shocked by the variety of colors.

I knew about Black, Blue, Grey, and Green. But Red, Brown, and—I walked over to the book next closest to me brushed my hand against it—Violet were new to me.

Pamela hefted the grey book. "This one says 'magic' on it."

I moved around the table, taking in each book, memorizing the color that was attached to it.

Winged: Blue

Fanged: Red

Furred: Brown

Magicked: Grey

Blooded: Violet

Psychic: Green

Demons: Black

Pamela flipped each book open to pages that were marked with scraps of paper.

"Do you think the colors have anything to do with the groups?"

"I don't know. Probably. There is very little coincidence in this world, things happen for a reason, not just for shits and giggles."

She gave a shaky laugh, and I really looked at her. "What is it?"

With a shaky finger, she pointed at the open page in front of her. "The words, I can feel them under my skin, like ants, moving." She scrubbed her hands over her arms.

Gods be damned, what the hell had Jack opened up here?

"Go over to the door, just stay there and keep an eye out for Jack."

She didn't argue with me, just backed away from the table and the books, kind of like how I wanted to.

I didn't really want to read what these books said. Not really. But that was the only way to find out what the hell was going on, because I seriously doubted Jack was going to come clean. Even once he saw the less than subtle B&E.

I moved to the book that Pamela had said made her skin crawl, the Green one, and read the page Jack had marked. Reading was slow going with the hand-written script, and I found myself reading the words aloud.

"Thus shall one Tracker stand between Orion and the darkness he brings. She shall be either our destruction or our salvation. No matter the outcome, her blood will be taken, drained to the last drop." What the fuck? Chills raced along my spine, my skin rising in gooseflesh I couldn't control. This was not sounding good. But, again, why wouldn't Jack want me to read this, unless he thought that the 'she' was . . . shit, he didn't think this was about me, did he? Yeah, it looked like I'd more than stumbled on Jack's deep dark secret he'd been keeping.

The Grey book came next and my heart leapt higher into my throat with each word.

"Orion shall twist the magic of the Great One, and shall bring her to her knees with his lies. For when he possesses the heart of her soul, salvation shall fall to one bound by oaths to stay his hand of death over the world. The Tracker must break her oaths to save the world, or we will all be doomed."

"I don't like the sound of that. It sounds like the Tracker could be you." Pamela's voice softened with each word, echoing what I was thinking.

This was too close to sounding like it was about me. Like these were prophecies for each of the different groups of the supernaturals, and maybe they all were about me. No, that couldn't be. I was Immune, there is no way they could Read me. So this was just stupid.

My fingers traced the words, and with each touch, my gut clenched and I fought to keep myself standing there. Stupid or not, I knew that I was staring at pages that would change my life.

"Yeah. Let's not jump to conclusions." I kept my tone smooth, but inside I was doing my best not to freak out.

Fuck, fuck, fuck! Each word from the books resonated with me and I couldn't deny that they felt as if they were directed at me. I made myself go slowly, so I wouldn't trip over my feet scrambling to get to the next book.

Blue, the Winged supernaturals.

"And our wings shall carry the Tracker into the final storm, and together, bound by blood, they will battle Orion."

Brown book, the Furred.

"The Great Wolf shall howl the Tracker's name, and claim her as his own, and shall spill his blood for her. And the Tracker will teach the submissive to stand; to shift and fight alongside her as Orion's darkness rises."

I gripped the edge of the table, struggled to keep my breathing even. No need to have Pamela wigging out. I skimmed the words again. These couldn't be true, couldn't be. I was Immune; they couldn't have read me. This was about someone else. They had to be about someone else. Teeth clenched, I shook my head. Maybe other people could lie to themselves, but it wasn't one of my talents.

"Rylee, I think Jack is home." Pamela whispered, peeking around the edge of the door.

I barely registered her words, so stuck on what I was reading. Fuck, how could this be about me? But what other reason would Jack have in hiding them from me? Moving sideways, I stepped in front of the Red book. The one attached to the Fanged.

"The Tracker will bring the Teeth together, making the mouth whole that it may bear down on the black rising horde with all its venom. For together, our bite will destroy all in our path." Not much better, maybe a little if only because I had no idea what Teeth were, or why they'd be brought together.

One more book.

Violet, the Blooded group. That made no sense to me; I would have thought Blooded and Fanged would be the same thing. I flipped the pages until I found a heading that actually made my heart stutter, the words wavering in front of my eyes, echoes of Giselle's voice whispering through me.

In my hands, I held the Blood of the Lost.

ABOUT THE AUTHOR

Shannon Mayer is the *USA Today* bestselling author of the Rylee Adamson novels, the Elemental series, and numerous paranormal romance, urban fantasy, mystery, and suspense novels. She lives in the southwestern tip of Canada with her husband, son, and numerous other animals.